Books by Molly Mack:

"The Storm Witch."

"The Bride of Vigon."

"The Streen." (Mike Cooper)

The **Bride of Vigon** was first published in 2024 by Malvern.

20 George Street, Kirkwall, Orkney KW15 1PW

2mikecoop@gmail.com

Copyright © Molly Mack 2024

Illustrations and cover by Mike Cooper

Copyright © Mike Cooper 2024

Printed by Amazon (Paperback & Kindle).

All rights reserved. No part of this publication may be reproduced, stored in a retrieval system, or transmitted in any form or by any means, electronic, mechanical, photocopying, recording or otherwise without the prior permission of the publisher. Nor be otherwise circulated in any form of binding or cover other than that in which it is published and without a similar condition including this condition being imposed on the subsequent purchases.

The Bride of Vigon *is set in the island of Yell, one of the most northerly Shetland Islands and is based on a **true story** from early 1800s.*

Many of the characters are real and events researched from recorded history are related in good faith. Some names have been changed and a few probably never existed. However, I have tried to keep within the boundaries of possibility.

This unique and intriguing story is embellished with my own interpretation of an extraordinary tale and therefore the novelette reads as fictional.

I have tried to reproduce the atmosphere of Shetland in the 1800s and use local accents and words where possible. To keep the story flowing I have tried to ensure the 'spoken' words can be understood with relative ease, so may not be fully accurate when read by the Shetland purist. However, I hope this will be a gentle introduction for those who wish to understand this unique Scandinavian influenced dialect.

I offer my apologies unreservedly should any of the characters, events or the language have any cause to offend.

Enjoy.

Molly Mack

The Bride of Vigon

Molly Mack

Malvern Books

For wir Bairns

The Cave

Hunched up with arms wrapped around her cold legs, chin resting on damp knees, Barbara watched the grey sky open up and transform into an artistic backdrop as the last rays of sun melted into yellows and pinks, and gently disappear behind the magnificent cliffs of Aastack. This was a really special place with many beautiful memories. Some lonely hours however had also been spent in these damp surroundings; watching, waiting, weeping.

The northern islands of Shetland seem to attract the worst weather during winter and over thousands of years, wind and waves have shaped the coastline into some of the most dramatic in Britain. Magnificent sea stacks stand aloof as they guard the entrance to thundering dark caves that have been carved into the rock face by centuries of northern gales, most of which can only be accessed by boat. One particular cave is well hidden under the cliff banks in north west Yell; no one apparently comes here or even seems to know about its existence despite it being less than a mile from the nearest house.

As an exploring eleven-year-old, Barbara had been collecting eggs from the cliff edge, (much against her mother's instruction) and she had followed a narrow sheep track down the grass slope winding between angry slippery rocks. A few rabbit bones littered the narrow ledge and crunched under foot, adding to her belief that no-one ever ventured here; the cave entrance was totally obscured until her final few steps revealed this very special place. Her mum had once mentioned a local smuggling tale and Barbara was sure the cave would have played a part in days of old. However, her mother never elaborated on the story and Barbara was too scared to ask in case her secret place might be revealed. Throughout her youth the cave became a regular hideaway where personal treasures were secreted and was a place where she would feel secure when her father raged his anger. The local fireside legends of Fairies and Trows were very real and came alive in the quiet darkness of the cave. It was strangely comforting to know she was not totally alone, and the mythical residents welcomed her presence when spoken to quietly. More recently it was a special, very private place where romance was explored.

She now sat shivering and wondering how things were going to develop. Barbara had been impulsive as a child. Her brother Magnie was eighteen months younger and stood head and shoulders above her, but he was the cautious one. He didn't join his sister on her clifftop egg hunts and could never make a decision. "A peerie bit less o' wan and a bit mair o' da t'ither wid be the makin' o' you both", their mother would preach many times as they grew up.

"Oh God what have I done this time" Barbara now said to herself in a whisper as she rocked back and forth.

Something disturbed a scarfie sitting on the cliff edge and with a few panicky flaps of oily black wings, it launched itself into a controlled dive amongst the surf below. She inhaled a quick silent breath and shrank back into the darkness as tiny stones were dislodged and rained down past the cave entrance.

Someone was approaching.

One.

This was a huge step in James Sinclair's life and only a few days left to go. Packing everything he might need for a year or more into one bag seemed impossible. In fact, he was becoming increasingly daunted by the whole prospect of leaving Shetland for the first time. Uncle Jake had spun romantic tales about the old clipper sailors squeezing their life's possessions into a large trunk before setting off around the world, "just in case they might find love and fortune and no' want to come back home!"

He had signed up in Lerwick twelve months ago and James had been informed at the time by the agents that "a canvas bag, no heavier than two stone is all that is permitted on-board the whalers. On top of this, the Company will supply oilskins at a discounted price, to be deducted from your first month's wage."

Getting essentials together for an Arctic winter or two at sea had been very difficult. The Yell shops stocked little other than basic needs, and even if they had what he needed the price would probably be far beyond affordable. So begging and borrowing from friends and neighbours was the only way. It had been hugely uplifting when visiting the Cullivoe shop to find a pair of boots in the back store that fitted well (with two pairs of socks on). Happy Harry, as everyone called him, had dug the boots out after half an hours searching "I kent dey were here somewey Jaimie. Them old leather things have been here since afore my faether died, so dey'll be a few years old noo, but still good as new… never been worn. Ha Ha!" laughed Harry living up to his nickname. "They will need a long steep in linseed oil tae soften up. Good sea boots though".

"Trust dee tae come up wae da very thing Harry, I will ging hame right noo and get dem sorted out. Hoo much do I owe?"

"Jest du taak dem awa. A couple o' salted whale steaks when du gets back hame will be payment enough…Ha Ha Ha!".

"Yon is more dan generous Harry. Thanks so much. I'll scarper afore du changes dy mind".

Having scraped a living at the fishing, just enough to keep him in food and ale since leaving school, James had no spare money and this was the very reason he had made the big decision to up sticks and give whaling a go. As soon as his intentions had been announced, donations of clothing and other essentials came pouring in, some more useful than others. The generosity of neighbours and friends was overwhelming and James vowed to repay them all on his return.

On his route home James stopped past his old mentor uncle Jake, who lived in the cottage called Grip. "I should have paid mair attention at school," he said as another re-fill frothed into his ale mug "I didna need an education to catch fish… but I should have listened tae da teacher. He said I had the brains to go on further, but I didna hae da wit tae listen. Aye, sailing da seas will be good. Navigation, dat's whit I widd really like tae do, Jake, if only I had paid mair attention at school".

"Aye James boy, du canna go wrong wae a bit o' learning. Du's a clever lad, tak some books wae de and get yon brain working again. Never look back boy, always look forward. Drink up look, dey'll no be much ale north o' da Arctic circle".

The northern part of Shetland was cold and wet at the best of times. However, the seas around Greenland would be something else, so taking advice from old Jake, who had spent a few years of his youth sailing to far latitudes, was essential, and between swigs of warm ale, they together compiled a list of essentials to pack into the kit bag:

- × *Shetland wool polo neck gansey and one for spare.*
- × *Four pair of thick socks.*

- *Long drawers.*
- *Two Simmits.*
- *Two pair of dungarees.*
- *Two woollen hats.*
- *Gloves.*
- *Four good flannel under shirts.*
- *Scarf.*
- *Two pair of water proof well-greased leather boots.*
- *A nit comb.*
- *A pocket knife.*
- *Paper and pencil.*

"Tak plenty tobacco James boy. Nothing so good as a smoke when frozen tae the core and hungry and nothing barters so weel when du needs a favour or a freend".

He was a great story teller was old Jake and had been the instigator in James's decision to go to the whaling. "Du'll hae the time o' dy life young Sinclair, an mony a tale will come back hame tae bore dy grandbairns".

James settled down for the evening beside a glowing peat fire. Jake lifted the lid from the wooden kirn and scooped another jug of ale. "The whaling will be da makin o' dee Jamsie boy." He was pouring the cloudy golden brew into white enamel mugs as a crack of wind rattled in the roof.

"Did I ever tell dee aboot da time we stopped tae tak on water in Rio……?"

The door swung open with a thundering crash; billowing skirts and a scream filled the tiny room as Peggy, Jakes widowed sister who lived next door, burst through the doorway. Confusion ensued for a brief moment as the two men jumped to their feet. "Come Jake, come noo, dere's tragedy arriving in Gloup da night, come and help. Jamsie, come doon tae da shore".

"Haud back a while Peggy. Whit's dis all aboot lass? What the hell's on wae dee?"

Grip was near to the burn and only a few hundred yards from Gloup beach. However, cooped up in the tiny stone house, the two ale drinkers had been unaware of the strong unseasonal wind that had rapidly built itself up into a gale. Jake grabbed his jacket and followed on behind Peggy. James, stumbled down the steep gravel beach and on to the sand, the wind stinging his eyes into tears. Six or seven women could be seen bunched together looking and pointing out to sea and a number of men were running towards the headland on the other side of the voe. "Hoo mony boats are still oot dere?" Jake shouted across to the huddle.

It was immediately obvious that any boats at sea were in imminent danger as the increasingly strong wind was blowing onshore, the tide was going out and waves were breaking on the shallow outcrops. A swell was running high and would create huge over falls at the entrance to the voe. Jake and James hung on to each other as they leaned into the wind. "Dis ebbing water will mak conditions impossible for da boats to come in safely. Hell I hope dey might have seen this coming and hae managed tae divert doon tae Cullivoe Da sea will be horrendous doon Bluemull Sound as the tide turns, but they might fare better than if dey try tae land on da beach here in Gloup."

"Two boats cam in a blink ago and are already hauled up in da noust. So dere's three still out dere. It'll be disaster; da swell coming in is huge. Look noo, see oot yonder, dey'll broach in yon braaking waves. Oh whit can we do?" Peggy yelled as she ran down towards the huddle of women.

When daylight arrived next morning it did indeed reveal disaster: one of the Gloup boats had been approaching the voe against the tide when the gale force wind arrived. Already cold and tired, the oarsmen were unable to control their heavily laden boat and broached, capsizing in the tumbling breaking sea, in view of their homes and family. Three of the four fishermen were lost that night in one of the worst disasters for many years. The other two boats had miraculously managed to fight against all odds and weathered the tidal gates of hell down to the relative security of Cullivoe.

Two.

The Lairds three story house stood high above the village of Gloup overlooking the voe, its large windows facing the northern panorama of summer sunsets. Nestled out of sight under the brae, small stone-built houses sat gable-on to prevailing winds. A large store house presided over the east end of the village where Josie Gray the Factor lived, keeping his eye on fish landings, making payments for quality cured fish and collecting most of it back again in rents.

Standing a few paces back from the window of the Haa, John Lawson watched the funeral group winding its way along the sheep track towards the kirkyard. "Such a disaster for our small community; another three men gone, two more widows with bairns left to fend for themselves. No doubt they'll be chapping at my door before the month's end looking for handouts. One less boat means our fishing income will be down this year again, not good not at all good."

Looking across the room, his wife sat engrossed with her embroidery, obviously not listening to a word. "I was saying Elizabeth, wool is fetching a good price these days. My father always said he would never go that way, not good for the community he said. However, it's getting harder to maintain a comfortable life and I may have no choice when the market price for fish decreases every year. Sheep. What do you think my dear?"

Elizabeth never looked up from her stitching, "I believe you will do what you want to do without my approval John. My opinion has never altered your business plans before so do what you must, just don't involve me."

At the back of the cortege James followed on silently, deep in thought as others up ahead talked in hushed tones following the coffins in sombre single file. Looking down over the heather and grass towards the voe he could see big brown wings of a bonxie swoop across the sea looking for its next meal. "*Such cruel birds, killing other birds to feed their young... I suppose that is just what we are all doing; eating to keep alive. For what ends I wonder, what's the big picture? Eat, work, sleep, die...Those poor families. What will they do now? It all seems so pointless sometimes.*"

"James" a whispered voice drifted over the stone wall as the procession passed the Lairds house. "Ower here James…"

"Babs?" James stopped with his ear bent towards the high wall as the others trundled on carrying their heavy burden. Side stepping through the gateway he stared "Babs, what's wrong? Why's du here? Du'll get the heave if yon Laird catches dee."

"I ken, but I need to speak. I need to see dee James afore du leaves. When is du coming to say cheerio? Du wis planin tae come past I hope, James? I'm worried I'll ever see de again James. I'm goin tae miss dee something bad."

"I can't stop noo Babs, du kens I need to be at dis horrid burial and den on to da wake. Women canna come to da drinking bit."

"I wouldna want to be dere anyway James among yon drunken rabble. Death brings such poverty and misery to the family, it shouldna be celebrated. If du bides sober du might want to come ower to Vigon later. We will have the house to wirselves. I'm going home for a few days and mam will be working here at da big hoose till da Laird leaves next week. Faeder will be too drunk as usual to walk home so he'll bide here in Gloup for anidder twa days at least."

"Ok lass, I'm been needing a yarn and to see de alone. I'll try tae leave da wake by good time, bit ging you back tae da big hoose noo."

It had been a long evening with many jugs of ale consumed. Grip was invaded by mourners and because it was more than a year since the last wake there were a huge amount of tales to tell and plans to plan. Saturday turned into Sunday and James sat looking at another large mug of ale balanced on top of an upturned fish box. Half asleep and not really listening to the drunken chatter, he was aware of daylight appearing through the tiny windows and slowly raised himself to his feet. Standing up he staggered a couple of steps and stopped beside Barbara's father Sam, sitting at the table with a mug in each hand. "Don't think I can hold anidder drap. I'm ready for home."

"Hear thish everybody...." slurred Sam, "Da Whaler boy canna keep up wi da men. When I was a bairn we would drink buckets o' ale and sometimes a drop or two o' da spirit and still be first doon at the boat to catch da morning tide. Fishing was hard, but we were harder....eh lads?" Nobody answered "Ach you're all saft in da heed. Wan yet afore you gang hame James boy..."

"Naa, I'm no gan' to waste anidder day Sam. I need to pack me bag yet. Da boat leaves for Lerwick in twa days."

"Ah yes... Whaling." Ale spilled down Sam's front as he drank, "No many folk come hame fae dat without a sore heart and often wae a sore arse, if du kens whit I mean. Ha ha!" Looking around everyone was avoiding catching his eye as usual. "I'll no see de afore du goes so tak care and mind on tae bring ush back some stories tae match old Jake over there's brave tales."

James didn't answer Sam's, sarcastic quips. He was best avoided when the drink was in control. A fiddle was being plucked in the corner and the wake looked set to carry on for a long while yet, so James figured he would not be missed and now was definitely a good moment to make his move. Adding an extra couple of staggers before arriving at the door to ensure everyone was convinced it was indeed time for him to go, he waved a farewell, "See ya," and closed the door behind him.

Three.

Even by local standards Vigon was remote. Two miles from Gloup, on the north western extremes of Yell, following sheep tracks on foot over heathery hills you will find the croft of Vigon.

James set off across sandy narrows at the head of Gloup Voe, wading through the shallow waters. His head was in a fog from a whole evening drinking strong ale. "Pleenk", as everyone called it, was for daily refreshment and bairns. However the stronger ale was kept for special occasions such as weddings and wakes. It had definitely not been the thinner pleenk version this evening!

Once up onto the hill he sat down to empty squelching boots and wring out his socks. He had navigated the lower sheep track to Vigon in the dark many times before so it should have been easy to follow on this calm April morning, but keeping focussed with a spinning head made everything much more difficult. The peat-based track was unexpectedly slippery in parts thanks to a heavy dew that sparkled in the rising morning light and a stumble could be at the very least painful and breaking a leg would be the end of his dreams to join the whaling this year. So very carefully with water logged boots, James picked his way through the heather.

A thatched roof eventually appeared over the peat bank as he approached Vigon and a tiny wisp of smoke from last night's hearth drifted up into the morning sky from the darkened house. James stopped as he neared one of the stone buildings. His feet were sore and blistered and he was out of breath; leaning against a low dyke he again removed one of his boots and peeled off the damp sock. A noise made him duck down. Old Jessie was walking in his direction... *"Oh god, what might she be up to at this time of morning…. old beesom".* Barbara's aunt Jessie lived in a tiny one-room building in the field below Vigon. A converted neep shed, it could hardly be called a house, but Jessie and her dogs had lived there for many years, helping to run the croft.

Jessie had never married and had no bairns, but was a valuable part of the community with her midwifery and other caring skills. She was also the best source of gossip for miles, so not the most welcome person to meet at four o'clock in the morning. She tottered across the track close to where James crouched holding his breath. Her steps grew faster as she approached, but turning to briefly look behind, her bright red scarf flew away in the morning breeze. "Oh damnation" she said as it disappeared over the peat stack. Only a stone's throw from certain discovery James shut his eyes and waited. However, Jessie abruptly turned into the kale yard and ducked down behind the grass covered earth mound. "*Ah, early morning call of nature*" noted James as he picked up the scarf and quietly scuttled unseen towards Vigon.

James knew Babs would be alone in the house so quietly lifted the latch and sidestepped in through the door without knocking.

"I hup yons no da Selkie man I hear yonder"

"Du might get a lot worse than a selkie man chappin' at da door this time o' da morning, just ax auntie Jessie. Thir's stories aboot her. She wisna free o' entertaining a selkie man or two in her younger days".

Barbara's bare feet clapped on the stone floor as she ran into open arms, "James, Oh! my god, here at last. Hell! it's been a while".

"I'm well honoured da night Babs, God and Hell in wan sentence. Last time I heard both o' dem mentioned was a fiery sermon fae some visiting minister in da pulpit!"

Barbara stood still, holding James at arm's length, looking into his eyes. Her long, slightly grubby nightdress hung low over cold shoulders. "I'm sorry about me goonie James. I don't usually welcome visitors dressed like dis, it is no even white anymore, but it is clean though." The last embers of a peat fire highlighted her long curls as she stood, shivering slightly, waiting for her clandestine visitor to make the next move

James looked around slowly, taking in the whole picture. Dreams had been many these past few months. He would be leaving Babs, his family and his home because a promise of good fortune was beckoning. A tear rolled down his cheek as he knew this was probably his last visit before departing. He offered her his hand and without a word they moved towards the bed.

It had been daylight when James arrived but the curtains were still drawn shut. As Barbara opened her eyes she knew it was unmistakably long past her normal rising time. Gently sliding down onto the floor to ensure she did not disturb the quietly snoring James, Barbara silently picked up some clothes and made her way out of the room, pausing in the narrow hallway to don shoes, breex and a gansey. Bright sunlight shone through as she opened the outside door. It was obviously past mid-day already, so daily chores were way behind: hens had to be let out, the sheep should be checked and the old cow needed to be milked. Aunt Jessie tended to the livestock most days, but she knew Barbara was home and so the animals would have been left to her attention.

Still feeling light headed from last night and with a broad smile, she gently closed the door behind her and faced the day with a much lighter step than she had experienced in months.

A recognisable voice drifted across from the byre where the door stood wide open.

"Hi Babs, no lik de to be late. I've fed da animals…the boggling was dat loud I towt I'd sort dem first and den come past to see if du was all right…?"

"I'm fine Jessie. Just makin' the best o' havin' naebody home…. a long lie is good once in a while!"

"Aye, I hear de! Your James is gaan tae da whaling I hear. He's a fine boy and will be a miss. I hup du will be saving body and soul for when he comes hame and gae us aal a fine wedding tae look forward to."

"Thanks for feeding da animals Jessie, and dinna worry, du'll be da first tae ken if I ever need tae think aboot marriage, bit it is no something dat will be happening for a while yet." Barbara wondered how long her old aunt might have been lingering outside the house before feeding the animals. However the old bird was also very devoted to the family and hopefully if Jessie knew more than she was saying, the secret would be safe…. for now.

Stone built 'but and ben' cottages were standard in the 1800s; 'But' was the kitchen end of the house where cooking, eating and living took place and a box bed would have formed part of this room, built against the partition wall. 'Ben' was a bedroom in the other end of the cottage, where clothes were stored and where visitors slept. However, visitors did not often frequent Vigon. The closet was a narrow passage, (sometimes forming a tiny bedroom) dividing the two rooms.

A new trend began in the early 1800s when houses were enlarged to display an element of wealth. Often after winter gales had demolished an old thatched roof, the opportunity was taken to heighten the walls and a cottage would be re-roofed to provide additional upstairs rooms. A steep ladder would be added to the closet and a cottage became a house. Vigon had two attic bedrooms added when Barbara was a young lass, providing more accommodation than many houses in north Yell. Since growing up Barbara now slept 'but', which was the warmest room in the house. Merran, her mother slept 'ben' and her father was confined to the closet, where he often stayed for days.

Barbara turned and strolled innocently back towards the house, calling back over to Jessie just in case she might follow. "I'll clean out da byre and come ower later on wae yon red scarf, I found it lying on the table this morning, how it got there I don't ken… anyhow, I'll be ready for a cup of tea then".

"Babs, Babs" called James.

"Shoosh……Jessie will hear de. She's in da byre and I tink she is already suspicious. I bet her lug will be pointed dis way." Barbara placed a couple of peats on the tiny glow in the open fire, poured milk and water amongst yesterday's bursten and stirred the pot. Looking for a jar of honey in the press she glanced with a smile over her shoulder at movements in the box bed. "Breakfast is comin".

James rolled across the bed and propped his head on the bolster which now hung over the wooden edging. He watched shards of daylight illuminating Babs auburn hair, as she busied herself at the fire. "Babs" he whispered, "Babs, I hae a problem".

Barbara turned and their eyes met. "What's wrong Jamesie"?

"It's cowld in here Babs. I need company…"

"Weel I suppose I can set da pot aside for a blink…it's no boiled yet. How could a poor peerie lass refuse an invitation like dat?" Without losing eye contact she slipped the shoulder straps down over her shoulders, stepped out of the old working breex, and moved across to James. He took her outstretched hand and quietly slid the box bed doors behind her.

Four.

The Linga was berthed at the jetty in Mid Yell, loosely tied halyards gently tapping the tall mast as she rolled in a gentle swell. The weekly supply of essentials had been discharged and the ferry boat would be sailing south to Lerwick on the flood tide as soon as the usual mixed return cargo including eggs, salt fish and mutton were loaded on board. James strolled along the quayside where everyone seemed to be busy… some more than others he mused. Stopping a while, perching on the corner of a low stone wall to view the comings and goings, he watched a stooped, slow moving figure making his way along the pier road, a cloud of smoke trailing behind. This would be old "Twenty Questions" as he was called locally, and James readied himself for interrogation as the shuffling male approached. A shout came from a window across the road "James, da very man…. come ower here, there's a dram waiting."

"Well that was a narrow escape. One interrogation missed, another about to begin", James said to himself, recognising the voice. "Robbie", James shouted as he strode across the track, "I was looking for de…when's du sailing?"

"Come ower here for a snifter James boy. We can speak inside."

Robbie Nisbet was the owner and skipper of the cargo boat Linga, which made regular trips with essential supplies to and from the northern isles of Shetland. Robbie was sitting in front of an open window watching the activities on the pier and he stood up as James came in the room. Pulling the cork from a bottle of rum, he waved it at James and set two glasses on the table. "Sit down boy and tell me what's happening in North Yell."

"I guess du'll hae access to mair gossip dan me Robbie. I'm no' been far fae da house for months."

Robbie poured two large shots and raised his glass. "Good health." One gulp later he refilled his own and sat down on the opposite side of the table. "Straight to the point James Sinclair… Been hoping to catch up dis past while. I'm getting owld, me joints are stiff and I hae no bairns."

"Let me think aboot dis Robbie. I don't ken any way tae stop getting owld, as far as stiff joints go I could fetch dee a staff and some o' grannie's liniment tae help de get a bit more mobile. However, I definitely can't do anything aboot da latter problem", James offered with a huge grin.

"Aye, I hear de", Robbie said with a smile... "Da point is; I'm looking for a good man to help me run da boat. I have been thinking aboot dis for a while and du's a perfect fit. We could work together for a year or twa and du might end up owning and skippering da boat. She's well found and earns good money plying aboot the islands."

"Well well Robbie, dis is not what I was expectin'. I'm speechless. Du's no dat owld yet and hopefully no too big a hurry. Why me? I'm sure dere's plenty idder folk wid jump at da chance tae go into partnership wae de".

"Du's a hard working lad and has a braaly good heed fixed on. I'm fairly confident du would mak it work. I have naebody to leave da business tae and a few folk are already been sniffing around, offering tae buy me oot. No chance o' dat. Having you as a partner wid gae a clear message tae keep off me patch. It sounds selfish, bit to even have a rumour at dis point will keep the pressure off me for the short term. It's for all da good reasons though as I don't want to see my years o' hard work building up the trade go to waste. I've been serving da peerie communities at a cost dey can afford and still make a profit. Yon sharks are looking for easy money and will offer nothing in return."

Robbie looked across the table and took a long swig of rum.

"Dere could be a good living here for years tae come for dee and a family, if du wis minded! Dat's me spiel James. What dis du tink?"

"God man dis is a lot tae take in." James stood up and paced around the room for a few silent minutes and sat back down on the wooden chair, picking up his empty glass. "Opportunities like dese dinna come along very often. I'm no sure whit tae say. I'm no sure I hae da heed for business. I need anidder dram."

James lifted his refilled glass to the window and looked at the watery sun through its dark contents for another silent couple of minutes. "Du'll have heard I'm off tae da whaling I guess Robbie?"

"Aye."

"Den du'll be looking for me to gie dat up for a start?" James asked tentatively."

"Don't be daft boy. In fact, the deals aff if du disna ging. Whatever discussions we hae the day is only the very beginning and I expect de tae fulfil all promises and obligations. Du signed a contract tae spend a season at da whaling and ging du will. Du wid regret no doing it for da rest o dy life and wid aye hae itchy feet. I'm no ready to step doon yet, but if we share da bones o a plan for da future I wid hae da satisfaction dat we both hae something to aim for. I can wait, even if it taks a number of years. As long as me health holds up den I will wait til da time suits!"

"Dis'll be a good tale for my wedding speech." James laughed. "I come asking da famous Captain Robbie Nisbet for a passage doon to Lerwick on his ald cargo boat an efter sharing a couple o rums I leave owning da company!"

"Haa! no so fast young man," Robbie chortled as he poured out the last of the bottle between them. "It'll be a lot o hard work and a few years yet afore dat bit happens."

"Ach I ken. I wis jus' pulling dy leg. It's a lot to tak in, especially when my heed is full o' idder tings. We can speak aboot it mair while we sail doon to da toon."

Captain Nisbet gave the Green Holm a wide berth as he lined up marks on the headland approaching the north channel into Lerwick Harbour. "Da narrow approach can be tricky if du disne hae wind and tide in dy favour", he advised James who was sitting on the port rail watching the crew working together tweaking sails and keeping the Linga on a steady course. The north easterly wind had been with them the whole run down from Yell and they quietly entered a surprisingly busy harbour before the sun began to set. Robbie was an excellent captain and had commanded ships across many oceans, of the world. However even he had to accept help from the berthing tug when parking his heavy sixty-foot cargo boat with its sails furled, alongside the harbour wall.

Lerwick, on the East side of Shetland was rapidly overtaking the old Norse capital Scalloway as the main harbour and industrial centre, and new construction could be seen all along the village front, replacing the old wooden slums of centuries. Stone jetties were advancing out into the deep water where nothing had been before, and small work boats were queueing up to discharge quarried stone and aggregates before heading back to Bressay for more. James looked on with wide eyes, amazed at how rapidly things had progressed since he last visited Lerwick only a year ago.

Robbie and James had spoken non-stop the whole trip south about their future business deal, and Robbie had even put pen to paper, with the bosun as witness. "Dat should make it legal withoot da expensive lawyer's stamp, God be willing" he declared, locking the wax sealed velum scroll in his cabin desk.

"So, tradition declares we hae tae "Maak aff the deal" James me boy and da alehoose across da road might be da place tae do it."

James was a bit overawed. This was so unlike the quiet skipper everyone knew. Old Robbie, like everyone else, enjoyed a good evening out, however during a working day would normally head off home as soon as they docked and his words were repeated to the crew every time they stepped ashore: "You go for a jug or two of ale boys. Here's a few silver pennies to get one on me, but just be sure to be here in the morning. Any man can sing and dance at night, bit it takes a real man to get up to work in the morning!"

Once settled into a quiet corner of the alehouse the new partnership raised yet another glass.

"Mind on Robbie", James pointed out, "I can only fully commit wance I get back fae da whaling. Du kens how it is. I might be a long while away, as wan year can run into two or three if we get stuck in da ice…"

"I ken James, dat's no problem. Get de clocking up da sea miles and study for dy mate's ticket when du has spare time." He raised his glass" Cheers to wis an a fine future."

James opened his eyes cautiously, waiting for the inevitable pounding head to arrive. Awkwardly rising onto one elbow he looked around, taking in unfamiliar surroundings; heavy window drapes blew inwards, letting enough daylight in to illuminate the dark red grain of a beautiful Canadian pine fireplace with rope and chain carvings running around the woodwork. A dramatic painting of a fully rigged ship in a gale hung above, "If dis isnae Captain Robbie's front room I'm a Dutchman", he said, quietly rolling off the long hard settee onto a bare wooden floor and groping around for missing boots. The door opened with a bang and a couple of seconds later the curtains were swept back with a single metallic swish. Robbie stepped in front of the window, casting his shadow on the startled figure of James sitting on the floor. "Time to get dy arse into action lad, Breakfast is ready an we need tae get underway. Dy boat arrived last night. She normally goes to Scalloway they tell me, however big changes are afoot and da ship is moored here on the East side."

The morning was bitterly cold with a fresh northerly wind driving showers horizontally through the streets of Lerwick village as they made their way through winding slippery lanes towards the harbour. James's health was not coping well with trying to avoid the overflowing sewers and he kept his handkerchief wrapped around his face. As they approached the wider shore road he stopped abruptly; a black cat, narrowly avoiding the hooves of a pony and trap, ran across and hid behind a stack of fish baskets. The wet and emaciated specimen watched them pass with only one eye open. "Oh hell Robbie I don't like dat wan peerie bit. It's a bad omen. Yon furry thing crossing wir path will bring bad luck."

"Och James min, I hope du's no serious. When du's oot on da high seas du'll need tae gi up da daft notions and superstitions dat ald landlubbers invented. Du'll gain da respect o' da crew if du can demonstrate logic ower old wives' tales. Be sure to show a grain o sympathy and understanding though, just to keep dem on dy side. Mark my words, dat bad luck stuff was invented as a means to blame idders for poor judgment and bad decisions. Witches were persecuted for centuries by fokk in power wha needed to bleem someen for dir own shortcomings an pure stupidity. Ach, du's gotten me going again. I could go on and on…sorry… Dat's me had my rant. I ken I'm an owld pain on dis subject; but da witch hunts are something very close to my heart and my family. I'll tell de all aboot it someday."

"Dinna worry Robbie, I ken whit du means. I didna mean tae offend. Dark days da witch hunts were indeed, and I ken whit du means when it comes to blame. There's none so ignorant as dem dat hae brains. I am really keen to learn more aboot local history because it's important and should be written doon for future generations. I'll be interested to hear all aboot your family tales when I get back."

A buzz was in the air as they rounded the corner, revealing a harbour front alive with purpose; women young and old were scurrying around in dirty wet unsuitable looking skirts, and rugged looking workmen pushing carts down the jetty with caps pulled tight over their ears were shouting and swearing at everyone. Three businessmen with tall black hats stood on the quayside looking out over the bay.

Most of the activity was directed towards two small flit boats tied alongside the newly completed stone pier. Water kegs and heavy boxes were lowered down and carefully stored in the bilges while salt fish, mutton and other foodstuffs would be loaded, once the rain stopped, and rowed out to the whaling ship "Hope", a large impressive three-masted barque anchored in the bay.

"Fine looking big ship oot dere James. Bonnie lines yon Peterhead built boats. She must be aboot ten years aald now and been a very successful whaler has the Hope. Made some good landings these past years I hear." Robbie stopped and gazed over the sea of heads milling around. "See yon three business men on da pier? Da lang wan in the middle is da local agent 'Head First.'"

"Head First? What kind o neem is dat?" said James looking at Robbie with a knowing grin.

"Aye, he doesna like being called dat though. His real name is Robert Slater, but at school he wrote his neem on his books as R. Slater and so he got the nickname Head First, Arse Later."

Robbie's laugh was so loud the men in suits turned to see the two of them wrap their arms around each other in fond farewell.

"Tak care noo young man and come back home wi dy fortune made an dy heed full o salty tales to entertain wis all."

"Never doot Robbie…I'll fin me way home."

Five

Babara was back at work in the Haa, feeling unusually cheery as she cleaned out the drawing room hearth, quietly humming a tune in time to the scrape scrape of her fire rake. She sensed rather than heard the floorboard creak. "Oh you startled me Mr. Lawson sir, I didna hear you come in".

"Don't stop Barbara. I do so like to see my staff happy at their work".

Barbara stood up, brushing the dust off her pinny head bowed she glanced briefly up at John Lawson. Normally an imposing figure, this morning he was dressed in a crumpled dressing gown, unshaven and looking rather older than his years. "Can I help you sir?"

"Not at the moment". He stood a while silent just looking. "Your Mr. Sinclair, I hear, has left for pastures new. Once he samples the excesses of the big wide world he probably won't return…they seldom do. You might be the one needing help."

As he turned and walked back through the door all she could hear was "Mmmmm."

"Oh mam, da Laird is gluffin me. Dat's da third time dis week he's come doonstairs in da morning and joost stands dere looking, speaks aboot James den gings."

"I ken Babs. Avoid him when du can and try never to be alone. I've heard stories aboot him and dey are no good. Joos think dysel lucky du dis mornings, I hae to do da evening shift!"

"At least he'll be away at da end o da week".

"Aye," Merran smiled. "His long suffering wife will be staying here at da Haa dis time, so we should have a few easy weeks. She's aye much more relaxed when he's away."

****

Glippapund shop was about three hours walk across the hills, and once a week Barbara made the journey to pick up supplies for surrounding households in Gloup and Westafirth. Flour was most essential, while salt, lamp oil, yeast and other bits and pieces were on the list, and bartering a few eggs or kale helped the budget.

The open freedom of the Yell hills had been part of Barbara's life since she was born. Appreciating such raw beauty during winter gales could be challenging, but she had grown up to thrive amongst the lands riches, even when there appeared to be very little to thrive on at times. The cliffs provided eggs and a few of the birds themselves could be salted down when the nesting season was finished. However, this was only done where it could be justified and sustainable. Barbara's knowledge and understanding of raw nature was huge. "Look after nature and treat it well and it will pay you back and look after you", her granny would say.

The trek up to Glippapund took you past many lochs and through peat bogs where danger lay should you be unable to read the terrain. "Keep to the old and long established pathway and don't venture out there at night" were words that Barbara heard in her head every time she made this journey. Granny Scollay used to tell a fireside story….an extra bit was added every time she told it:

> *"Owld Matty wis a crofter doon da sooth end o' Yell. He had twa sons an his wife Mary was a while younger dan him. In his youth Matty was a big strong man who could lift a barrel o herring above his heed, it took two men to lift it back down! He was a braaly good fiddler and was aye welcome at a foy.*

Wan particular night he was at a wake and had been drinking a muckle boady o ale wae aa da idders. Dere had been dancing and music gaan on weel intae da smaa hours. At some point, naebody kens when, Matty decided tae mak his way home. He could have geen along da road, aboot three miles, but surely took a shortcut ower da hill. Weel dis du you ken whit? When he got as far as da peat bank, dere in front o him sat a young lass on tap o a muckle hurd. Lang hair draped down ower very pronounced breests an wearing a sparkling blue dress Matty had never seen da like; der was something very unreal aboot da scene and anyhow… hoo did she come to be up here in da hill on her own?

"Oh my god," he said, "whit is du doing up here in da peat bank at dis time o' night lass?"

"Will you play me a tune Matty?"

"A tune…why should I do dat?"

"'Cause I'm told du can play a fine reel Matty." She held her head on the side looking him in the eye teasingly "Du has a fiddle under de oxter, and I tink du finds me a peerie bit attractive."

"I cannot deny du is a fine looking lass, but I need to be getting home."

"Weel Matty, I tink dat wild be a mistake. I could mak life very difficult for de and dy family if du disna come wae me da night"

At the mention of his family he picked up a stick and shouted: "Nae body threatens Matty Johnson or his family. Ging back whar du belongs, TROW, or I will show de whit difficult means!"

The beautiful vision jumped down from the rock with golden hair cascading behind and held out her hands towards Matty. He took a step towards her waving the stick aggressively above his head, "Du picked da wrong man tae pester dis time, TROW." But suddenly sliding doon da bank he was up tae his knees in murky peat bog water and slowly sinking. "Hell and damnation be wi you. Get me out of here."

As he looked towards the grinning figure daylight started to appear ower da hill behind and a shard o early morning sun shone through her locks. She turned and screamed...

Matty eventually scrambled his way oot o da peat bank and ran most o da way hom, cold and weet and he never saw his fiddle again.

Folklore tells us Trows cannot be oot in daylight, or dey become petrified. Dere is a standing stone up on da Hill of Canisdale to dis day...

I've been up dere and seen it, so you see it must be a true story!"

"Hi Babs. Not much o a day to be venturing oot lass" said Bessie as she was blown in through the shop door. "I saw de makan' doon the brae in dat last shower o' rain. Come in bye and I'll make wis a cup."

"Ah dat wid be good Bessie. Tink I might need some rest afore I venture back oot dere. Da wind is vicious. I should hae left my shopping tae anidder day."

Bessie hitched up her skirts and strode towards the door, then stopped. "Ah yes…" she turned back and opened a small cupboard door behind the counter and picked up the only envelope on the shelf and handed it to Barbara. "Miss B. Brown, Vigon, North Yell… I guess dis must be for dee lass. Sit doon while I ging through and boil da kettle."

Barbara's mouth opened but no sound appeared. She felt her cheeks warm. "Oh I wasn't expecting…"

"Sit doon and read dy letter lass. It only cam dis morning. I tink I can guess wha it comes fae! I'll be back in a blink".

Barbara's hands were shaking as she opened the grubby and water stained envelope. Lifting it to her nose she inhaled the smell of tar and hemp…

My Dear Babs.

I hope you are well.

We have been waiting in Lerwick nearly two weeks for the wind to move out of the west, but at last it has shifted back east o' north and we are ready to depart in the morning.

The "Hope", at 242 tons looks to be a fine whaling boat so please do not have any worries about her seaworthiness. I have met most of the crew now. Three others are joining from Shetland and we are all eager to get underway… Davis Strait first stop I think!!

A. Geary is the skipper and has a track record for making good landings, so am hoping for some healthy pay settlements.!!

I met up with Captain Robbie Nisbet on the way down and have some exciting news for when I return. However, there is a lot to think about and I hear the whistle blow, so must get my arse back down the pier. I will tell you all about it when I can.

I will write again soon, but god kens when I will be able to send it!!

Take care.

J. X.

Barbara's walk back home across the hills seemed to take forever. The back-pack straw basket was laden with shopping, her hands were cold, the load was cumbersome and the wet and windy conditions pushed her off the track every few steps. She felt no pain and was floating in the air, going over and over the memorised letter folded in her coat pocket. "Oh God, a whole year is going to be so long. I miss James so much already. Exciting news that involves Robbie Nisbet. what on earth can he be speaking about?

And a kiss…he left a big X for me…"

Six.

The passage across to Davis Strait had been uneventful, The 'Hope' made excellent progress across the north Atlantic and was approaching the southern tip of Greenland coast in a week.

April was bitterly cold and James had been advised to devote his spare time to making snow boots and clothing out of cured animal skins provided by the company. Captain Geary was very approachable and he introduced the most recent recruits to their new surroundings and duties. These included helming and encouraging them to learn basic navigation. James showed good promise from the start and was keen to learn how to use the sextant which can be a very difficult instrument to master. However, his persistent nature insured he picked up the basics after very little tuition. His ability and determination led him to be trusted from the very start and he was honoured to be invited to join the hunter boat as an oarsman when the first whale was sighted.

These small whale boats were very like the Shetland "sixareen" with six oarsmen, a helm and two harpooners. James was in his element in this boat and his strong arm and calm head ensured he progressed to helming in a matter of days. The chase often lasted many hours and was obviously the most important and toughest part of the whale fishing industry. Chasing whales in the open ocean many miles beyond the safety and support of the 'mother' ship was stressful; harpooning and making a kill and then towing the carcase was gruelling and backbreaking work. The seas were often rough and challenging; oarsmen became cold, tired and hungry and they could be working around the clock in the long Arctic daylight far from safety and support. After towing the great whale back to the "Hope" the process of flensing a carcase took place once it was tied and secured alongside. Huge blocks of blubber were hoisted up to the deck, further reduced in size and put into barrels, then stored in the hold to be sold and processed at home. The huge unused remains were then cast adrift and left to birds and other sea scavengers to feast upon.

Seas and conditions in general in these high latitudes are notoriously very unforgiving, and accidents are considered part of daily life. The Hope's surgeon, Angus, wanted to join the harpoon boat on one occasion, against the advice of captain Geary, so a long stand-off ensued between the pair. The captain however must have lost the argument and "Medical Angus" clambered awkwardly down the scramble net as the small boat wallowed alongside. Stepping onto the greasy gunwale of the lively boat, he immediately lost his footing and fell with wind-milling arms into icy waters. A textbook quick recovery thankfully saved his life but the saturated heavy wool clothing rapidly froze and ensured he spent many days in his bunk recovering from the cold shock. This near miss was a lesson to everyone and helped sharpen up some safety practices for a day or two. The nickname "Medical Angus" changed overnight to become "Mad Angus", of which he surprisingly became rather proud.

Weeks turned into months and the hold slowly filled up. However, captain Geary was not happy. Time was running out and more bowhead whales were needed to make a capacity loading. A successful trip depended on quality and numbers. They could risk going further north into the ice where getting trapped for the winter was a real possibility, but the gamble was that if the trip was cut short by a few weeks the market would be eager and the first boats to land would command the highest prices. What was already on board could possibly ensure a good profit for the season. A decision would be made soon.

James lay in his bunk braced against the constant rolling, looking into the darkness and listening to the shouting of men and the clanking of pumps emptying stinking bilges every three hours. He was getting increasingly disillusioned with what was happening, not just on board the "Hope" but the industry as a whole. He was able to cope with the long cold freezing days, where rest only came when the harpoon boats were hoisted back on board and they sailed a few hours in search of the whales. However, he could never accept the sheer scale of slaughter and waste involved; only half the carcase was processed for blubber and taken home to the markets. A very small amount of whale meat was used in the ships galley, however a huge part of the kill was discarded... hundreds of tons every season wasted, thousands if you added the whole north and south seas whaling industry together. The stench of the culling process and the barrels of blubber in the hold was unbearable. It saturated clothing and contaminated your very core. Young calves were often left motherless and followed the boat for hours and the hugely distressing sight of pregnant cows being mercilessly butchered tipped the balance for the young Shetlander. The dream had ended and James wanted to go home.

A month later his prayers were answered when Captain Geary announced they should batten down the hatches and make haste for Peterhead. The season had not been bounteous and tonnage was down on previous years, so assuming other ships would be experiencing the same problems it could be a race home to command the highest market price.

Helming and working the Hope to make best speed, James was in his element. Perfecting the sextant and mastering navigation, he felt at one with the ocean experience. Night sailing was a delight, when the whole world appeared to be asleep and he felt so alive and constantly gazed in awe at the canopy of stars, millions of stars that magically moved with the passing hours. Polaris, the most important beacon in the northern sky, remained fixed on the Larboard side as they pounded their way through the white topped swell. The course to Peterhead had been plotted to take them through the Pentland Firth, between the Orkney Islands and the north of Mainland Scotland, which was only a hundred miles from his home in Shetland. So heading back east James was feeling very content and a bit excited..

"I have had enough o whaling, it's no for me…" James said to the mate as he steadied himself against the big steering wheel, breaking a long silence. "I hope we all get a good pay for the trip but I'm really no sorry to be heading home."

"For Christ sake mon, what are you on about" replied the mate. "You're one of the best helms we have seen on board the Hope for a long time, you are a natural with the navigation as well. You canna waste that skill. Stick with it James mon, stick with it, you'll do well."

After landing her cargo of blubber on the Keith Inch quayside, the Hope tied up alongside Peterhead's inner north berth and the maintenance gang descended on to the deck to begin a much needed overhaul. James and a couple of the crew helped each other with their heavy kitbags on to the pier and stepped ashore to dry land for the first time in months. James's wobbly legs followed the others towards a queue forming outside the Agent's office where Captain Geary was waiting.

"Well James lad, we made a fine price for our cargo, so all in all it was a good decision to cut a bit short and get back before the other boats. You are a natural seaman, better than many we've had on the crew for a number of years I might add, so don't tell anyone but you will find a small bonus has been included."

"Thank you Cap'n. Much appreciated," James responded feeling rather humbled by his Captains words.

"I see you haven't put your name down for next season. I was kind of hoping I might be able to persuade you to join us again. There will definitely be a berth on board for you should you want... maybe you have something better on the horizon though?"

"I cannot tell a lie Cap'n Geary. I have immensely enjoyed da experience and da Hope was mair as I ever dreamed of. Da camaraderie o da crew was second to none and I have learned a huge amount fae yourself, I could never hae wished for better... so tanks very much. I am struggling though wae da whaling itsel and don't think it's something I could face again. Du will no be able to understand... but tanks, however regretfully."

"Aye, I did suspect that would be your answer and appreciate what you say. It's not for everyone. I have watched you struggle with the cull and flensing…not very pretty and I must admit to avoiding the worst of it myself." He looked at James with a long hard stare. "Mind though, as far as the crew are concerned I am a hard bastard so keep that to yourself…ok?"

"Aye of course Captain…"

"Don't give up the sea. You are a Sheltie and made of the right stuff. You'll do well if you stick in. I kind of predicted this, James, and took the liberty of contacting an old acquaintance. Do you know William Smith?"

"No… I don't think so", replied James very cautiously.

"He's a young lad, sailed with me a few years ago up to Greenland and on another whaling trip to Davis Strait. A damned good hand, a bit like yourself, James, and ambitious. Anyhow, he formed a partnership with a number of others two years ago. They had a cargo ship built in Blyth named the "Williams". She's tied up in Aberdeen looking for crew. I have here a letter of recommendation should you wish to join.

James was taken aback and sat in silence for a minute, not fully taking in what was happening. "I don't ken whit to say Cap'n. Dis is more dan I deserve. Are du sure? How can I ever thank you…?"

"Stop there James, It's no more than I would do for anyone who shows they have the mettle... Go for the chances life presents, my father and his father before him told me many times *"The only things you should regret in life are the things you never do"*. Don't be over ambitious though. Do what you can and do it well. The industry needs more like you."

James walked out of the office with the letter in his hand and six month's pay tucked into the sheep's leather money belt he had been given in Shetland. "When du's sooth" old wise Jake had said "du will mak mony freends and du'll meet mony no so friendly. Keep dy hard earned money wrapped tightly next to dy skin in dis belt, but ensure du haes some paper notes in dy pockets to keep appearance up. If du gets set upon dey will take da easy money and hopefully leave de wi dy fortune untouched. I ken what hits like to be rich for a day!"

A cold east coast breeze halted his breath as he stepped outside. No one was paying him any attention so he wandered along the street and sat down on cold sandstone steps in front of a locked-up butcher shop.

A few minutes later Mad Angus was standing in front of him with a big smile. "Well James me lad, waiting for the butcher shop to open?"

"I am confused Angus. I don't ken what to do next, Dere's a boat leaving Aberdeen for Shetland next week and dat's where I should be going. Home is where my heart lies and I need to ging back to where Babs will be waiting, but my heed says earn some more money first… Or is it da idder way round? My head says ging hom and my heart says go anidder trip. Och, du's da wise een Angus wi all dy medical learnings. Tell me whit I should do."

"I don't think love was part of my training, but I'm not against helping a shipmate. Follow me young man," Angus said as he strode across the street towards the Union bar. "What you need is some planning juice and the first one is on me…"

"Planning Juice…" James stood up shaking his head slowly and gently bumped his heavy canvas bag down three steps and across the cobbled road. "Now where have I heard that before?"

Seven.

Vigon hill was covered in a dusting of early season snow. Winters in Shetland were often long and seemingly never ending, and to have snow in early December meant it would be a long haul until spring. Barbara's father Sam, was becoming increasingly less interested in working the croft and would hide himself away for days, living off nothing much more than ale and bannocks. Barbara and her mum were only just keeping things together; working long hours at the Haa left them little time to work the croft and between them money was scarce. Sunday was the one day they were at home together and it was spent cleaning the byre, repairing wind damage around the house, washing clothes and generally preparing for the following week.

"Any word fae James?" Merran asked as they both struggled, arm in arm down the wet and slippery track at the back of Vigon towards the Whinnie Knows, where they suspected a couple of sheep might be hiding from the snow.

"For the hundredth time no," responded Barbara, a bit sharper than she intended, "Du kens I'll tell de when I hear…"

"Sorry Babs, I just hae dis aafil feeling something's happened."

"Oh midder I ken, sorry… I must keep up hope. It's been a difficult couple o' years wi nee word. I pray every night for his return. I spoke wi Robbie Nisbet a peerie while back and he tinks dat James will fulfil da deal dey struck aboot going into partnership and takin ower da cargo boat…it soonds a brally good offer. But oh dear, I'm beginning tae doot all dis religion stuff. Da minister tells me tae trust in God and I will hae nothing tae worry aboot…It disna seem to be working. However, better to pray every night just in case. Dou never kens."

"Aye, we hae tae live in hope. Hits been twa years noo though Babs."

"Robbie said da bowheads have been seriously depleted dese past years and boats are noo having to venture further north to fin whales and seals. Dey often get stuck in ice all winter, sometimes longer. He was trying tae play it doon bit did admit dat a number o boats had been lost in da ice. He said no tae worry, da Hope is a well found boat wi a good skipper and she has made good landings dis past while. He's likely geen back up north a trip. He might even have joined anidder ship Robbie said. He promised to ax aboot and see if he can fin oot onything."

"Peety he's no written tae dee though Babs. Just a peerie note wad do."

"I ken. But mind, da Aberdeen boat was wrecked last year and she was carrying da mails. His letter might have been lost." The tears were by this time pouring down her cheeks.

"Aye Babs, I hear de."

****

The harvest home supper was something everyone enjoyed and was held in a barn behind the Haa every October when most of North Yell were invited. The laird provided a feast and the community themselves contributed ale and music.

The staff at the Haa had been baking bannocks and preparing food all week, half a dozen sheep were prepared in traditional Shetland fashion and everything was falling into place for the evening ahead.

Guests arrived in dribs and drabs wearing their Sunday best. A dram of whisky for the men and a sherry for the women was given out as they entered the gaily decorated barn; brightly coloured bunting hung from every roof beam and a huge union jack flag covered most of the end wall. A buzz was in the air with conversation and laughter growing louder as the barn filled and the buckets of ale emptied.

The Haa staff were all dressed in domestic servant's uniform: black skirt, white blouse and pinny with a white starched bonnet. Merran and Barbara were in the line of servants carrying out dishes of bread, mutton, cheese, and much more from the kitchen across the courtyard and onto a big table below the union flag. A smaller table offered sugary delights; scones, cakes and jams never seen by anyone since last harvest home.

On their way back to the Haa with empty trays Barbara and Merran were stopped by the Laird John Lawson. "Fine night for the feast lasses. You're doing a grand job."

Merran nudged her daughter and whispered "Say nothing. I ken whit's comin…"

"Been three years now Barbara…three years." The Laird stood in front of them and stared across the voe for a few uneasy minutes. Edging up close and flicking his eyes across her cleavage he smiled. "You're getting on in years now lass. That waster you once had a notion on…James Sinclair… seems to have disappeared, flown the proverbial nest it seems".

He paused, waiting for a response, but none came.

"As your employer I am concerned for your welfare and for your future. Another pair of strong hands about your small croft would be welcome I have no doubt, especially the way your father seems to be struggling."

Barbara took a couple of steps back holding the silver oval tray higher in front with both hands. "Thank you for your concern sir. However we are managing fine".

"Charles Russland is a good man. He's not short of a few pounds either…might be helpful when the rents come due." Without waiting for a response he turned on his heel and strode into the darkness.

Merran wrapped an arm around Barbara, "Oh god Babs, he is a bully and I don't trust him. He has been pestering me for da last six months or more aboot da rent due on Vigon. I just don't see hoo we can manage…we are struggling."

"Oh Midder, I ken things are serious and da Laird has the power to do whit he wants. I'll do whitever I can to help make things better, I promise. James will surely be back soon and it'll all work oot."

"Only trying to help Babs. Da years are moving on and like he says…Charles Russland is a fine lad."

"Weel" said Barbara, "Dat's no gaan' tae happen!"

"Sorry lass, forget I said dat. I'm just all wound up. Look, we are aff duty noo til clearing up in da morning. Let's rid wirsels of dese trays and get back tae da barn, I hear da fiddles starting up. Forget owld Lawson for wan night. Come wae me. I hid a bottle of sherry ahint da millwheel".

As she turned Barbara caught site of Charles Russland leaning up against the barn door smoking a pipe and chatting to her brother Magnie. She heard rather than felt herself take a sharp intake of breath.

"Whit did du say Babs?"

"Nothing Ma…. let's find dat bottle".

Eight.

The first run across the North Sea was worse than anything James had encountered in the North Atlantic: short sharp seas had no pattern, huge lumps of water rolled over the stern totally unexpectedly and steering often required two on the helm. Within thirty miles of land the waves increased in size and were unpredictable, even in moderate winds. "Dis is no bad weather boys…gi me a good day off the Waast o' Shetland and I wager you'll be shouting for your midders to come and taak you hame," James was heard to say whenever things became difficult. He was hugely respected for his seamanship and was living up to a growing reputation of being an extremely good helm. Captain Smith would rightly brag up any crewman when they performed well. James was no exception. "Dam good man to be in charge of the deck. I can sleep without worry when James is up top". The crew might have taken exception to this newcomer, but were all very much in agreement and suitably impressed.

"I'm guessing it will be difficult to make profit on the North Sea runs," James tentatively suggested to his new captain one evening as they lay at anchor off Bremerhaven waiting for a pilot. "Week in week out the wind seems to be against us. Whatever direction we sail, we are constantly criticized for late arrivals. Every boat has to take a Pilot and Tug and we are constantly at the mercy of things beyond our control."

"Aye James, very perceptive. I think we are on the same page there," replied Captain Smith.

"You are fully aware we had the Williams built for some serious cargo runs and have done reasonably well on the North Sea trips, despite your concerns, but I am keen to move on. Keep this to yourself for the moment James, but we are moving on to carry some goods across to southern France and Portugal next month and my partners are pricing a contract to carry general cargoes to Buenos Aires. These Southern Ocean runs can be very lucrative and are sought after by the big companies, so it needs to be kept quiet for now. However, I've been meaning to speak with you... I think this might be the time to make you an offer. I need good reliable crew to venture across the equator and beyond, and you are making good progress with your tickets. I believe you would benefit from a few ocean passages as Second Mate. If all goes well it means a bonus at the end of each voyage on top of your new wage increase".

"Well, I think you might not have to wait long for my answer. Dis is very generous and I very much appreciate your confidence in me. I couldn't possibly refuse" said James without hesitation. "When wid we be departing, assuming you get the contract?"

"Once we return from the Portugal delivery we could be loading in Portsmouth and heading for South America within two months".

Despite his initial eager acceptance of the offer, James sat on the bottom bunk of his tiny shared cabin pondering. He hadn't been home for nearly three years and had been planning to ask for time off next month. He had written to Babs on a few occasions without response. That was to be expected as his mail address had changed with his new employment and any reply probably would never have caught up. He hoped she had at least received his letters. The most recent had never been posted and were still in his kitbag. He felt guilty, but also worried he might be giving out false hopes and promises that could never be fulfilled. James's new found career was more than he could have wished for and he was loving it, but was acutely aware his life and loves in Shetland were so far removed from what was happening today, and to fulfil his deal with Robbie Nisbet to take over the cargo boat was more a dream than a real possibility at this time. There was definitely no doubt he would eventually return to the islands of his birth once he got himself a healthy bank balance, he just wasn't yet ready. James stood up and opened a locker door below the tiny porthole window and withdrew a tin mug and a bottle of port. "Forgive me Babs, don't forget me. Du is in my heart and I will come back tae de."

****

The brig Williams was trading between the UK and South America for the next few years and became a highly respected and successful merchant voyager.

In 1818 they again set sail to South America carrying a substantial cargo that was bound for Valparaiso Chile. The mixed cargo contained musical instruments, hats, iron, books, confectionary and wine amongst other things. After a good Atlantic crossing they resupplied at Buenos Aires and sailed towards Cape Horn. As they sailed south, however, the winds increased dramatically and after some challenging weather past the Falkland Islands they were still unable to head west towards Cape Horn, so sailed much further south in search of more favourable winds to enable a turn towards the Horn.

On the 19th February they unexpectedly sighted land. James was on the helm at the moment it was sighted, and after some frantic sail reduction under the lee of its shores it was determined this was land that had never been charted. The crew unanimously agreed it should be called South Shetland Islands to honour James who had first cast eyes upon its shores and managed to avert a shipwreck by his quick action.

They hove-to overnight, then proceeded further south the next day when they sighted more land which was named Williams Point. They also sighted land later called Livingstone and Greenwich Islands. The weather and ice then dictated they move on and continue their passage around Cape Horn and north to Valparaiso.

On reaching Valparaiso Captain Smith reported the discovery of these islands to a senior Naval officer, who expressed doubts at the claim and thought that Smith had sighted ice only. Determined to prove the sighting the Williams departed again on 16th May 1819 and sailed south towards Cape Horn and the islands. However, the ice and winter winds during this southern winter ensured they could not navigate back to their recorded coordinates and they eventually turned north to Montevideo.

News of the discovery, however, had preceded them and the sealing ship Espirito Santo was soon bound for the newly discovered islands. Unfortunately, this became the first of many sealing expeditions to the South Shetland Islands over the coming decades.

The Williams spent the next three months in Montevideo carrying out repairs and gathering enough cargo for a return trip to Valparaiso. James spent much of this time helping with repairs and studying for his first mates ticket for which he now had more sea time than required for an exam.

After their long stay in Montevideo they again headed south, and by the 17th October the Williams was again sailing along the coastline of these newly discovered southern islands. King George Island, Nelson Island, Robert Island, and Greenwich Island, finally arriving again at Williams point. They then sighted new land which was higher than any previously discovered and named it Smith Island. Needless to say the crew were ecstatic and rum rations were broken out…celebrations were well deserved.

Finally arriving again in Valparaiso Captain Smith's claims were now believed by the Naval officer. The Royal Navy then chartered the Williams and installed their own captain and three other ratings. They made land on the 19th December 1819 and ran along the north shore of New South Shetland. They then ran to Deception island, sighted Trinity Island and the northern tip of the Antarctic Peninsula and continent. This was the first recorded sighting of the Antarctic continent in history.

The Williams was eventually halted by sea ice in the Weddel Sea after sailing past Elephant Island and Clarence Island and they finally arrived back to Valparaiso by April 1820 where it was confirmed the islands had been given the name "South Shetland Islands". Captain Smith was overwhelmed with the Naval reception and was praised for his exceptional seamanship in discovering, and his persistence in recording these islands in the Kings name. James helped ensure the party lasted most of a week in true Shetland style…it took another week to recover!

They made a fifth and final journey back to the islands on the way home, but eventually arriving in Portsmouth to find that Captain Smith's partners and fellow owners of the Williams were in financial difficulties and the company was bankrupt as a result. The Williams was subsequently sold, and together with a skeleton crew of eight, James helped deliver the boat to Newcastle in early 1823.

****

Leaving the ship was a huge wrench for all on board. Many of them had spent years together trusting each other, working and living in a relatively small area day and night, through calms and storms, highs and lows. Lifelong friendships were formed, and lives often depended on trusting your workmates when things, especially the weather, was against you. However, it is well recognised amongst the tars that not all bonding took place under sail; lots of pints and rums were consumed in the taverns once landfall was made and many tales and stories from those forays ashore could never be made public. They had been a good crew, and considered themselves a close knit family, but now an unknown future had been presented that would split and end the security and friendship that had bound them for so long. A very sombre group shuffled across the quay in the dark evening drizzle and deposited their worldly belongings, one by one, onto a trailer that was bound for the hostel where they would all spend a final night in Newcastle at the new owner's expense.

The Grey Horse, across the bridge was the nearest pub and offered enough room to seat everyone around one table to the rear of the inn. Captain Smith ordered eight pints of beer and eight glasses of porter which were duly delivered by a traditional bar wench. William Smith stood up and waited for silence. "Well, this is not going to be easy. Eight of us are here tonight and we are missing four that joined us for the Atlantic crossing home. However most of us sat around this table actually formed the core of our original crew that departed England in 1818. Amazingly we have all stuck it out together, through thick and thin and all that. Thanks to you all for everything, and I mean it. A huge thanks. Some of you have been with me for a decade or more... Effing idiots", raising a huge roar of laughter. "Hang on though... I mean it. What an amazing bunch you have been. I know I had to shout at times, I know you were doing your best even when I was shouting, but you never let me down. We have crossed oceans and seen some amazing sights, discovered new lands, achieved more than any average cargo boat could have dreamed about. You are without doubt the best crew I could have sailed with."

Captain Smith raised his glass and downed it in one as the team noisily pushed chairs back and got to their feet. "The Williams."

Everyone sat down but James stayed standing and looked across the table at the skipper.

"Hang on James boy... sit down", shouted Captain Smith. "You might be four years older but that doesn't give you any authority over me. Ha Ha..."

"William", James said as he remained standing with sober face "I have only called you by your first name once before (and that was a good few years ago now). It was to accept the position to join the crew. A bit cheeky at that point to call you by your first name I know, but I was nervous and naïve, so I now offer a belated apology! However, William, young man, now that we are no longer under your command we can say and do whatever we wish."

Huge laughs and clinking of glasses erupted.

"Hang on guys, tame down," James said quietly as silence arrived again. "What I really want to say is thanks. Thanks to this man, we have all had some of the best times of our lives. I don't intend to list all the good bits and definitely not the bad ones. But as a crew you have been outstanding. Maybe a bit rough and smelly at times, sorry Scrubber! Hang on a minute though guys, you were responsible for taking the Williams across seas where others have perished. I know da last couple of years especially, has been a voyage we will remember for the rest of our lives: Discovering new lands is something that doesn't happen every day and for me to be part of naming the South Shetland Islands is something that will be written into my family history for ever. So thanks, thanks again to Captain Smith for making it all possible and you the crew of the Williams for being part of a family we will never forget."

Captain Smith waited for silence. "Individual praises and bragging is not good. Everyone works together. We had a good gang and came together well as a team. OK, there were times of disagreements, sometimes fairly major ones I regret now, so I am sorry to anyone who might feel I was unfair." Looking across the expectant faces making no particular eye contact he took another gulp of beer. "Boys, we have been praised by others for our seamanship and fast deliveries, we wrote ourselves into the history books having discovered new lands, we helped the navy survey and draw up charts for future generations to navigate by. You have every right to be proud of yourselves and I am happy to give a reference to any of the crew who needs it for future employment. Well done again and despite the company's financial troubles, I hope what they were able to offer as a bonus will confirm full appreciation".

Another huge cheer filled the Public House.

"One last thing. I said that individual praise should be avoided, but have been asked by the crew to say something more. James…James here is someone the whole crew respect and admire. He was always there for everyone; however, he came to us as a second-hand whaler from the Shetland Islands…"

He waited patiently for the cheers and clinking glasses to stop.

"James joined the merchant trade as a disillusioned whaler as the suffering, pain and killing of intelligent life was not for him. So he joined the "Williams" where intelligence was not an issue."

The crew again roared with laughter and banged empty beer mugs on the table.

"Seriously though, this young Sheltie turned out to be the best and most trusted helm I have ever sailed with. He is a natural and respected seaman and we all wish him well for the future. I can also reveal, he doesn't know this yet, but after many months of study, training and ocean miles we can now call him Captain James Sinclair".

James stood up again amidst the shouts of congratulations. "I am totally overwhelmed boys…sorry, I am for once speechless. But thanks Captain Smith and thanks everyone. So, before anyone else comes with any more shite and speeches the next round is on me…Barman…double rums all round!"

Nine

Charles Russland had been a farm worker on the North Yell estate since leaving school at fourteen. He was hard working and been elevated to the position of head shepherd the previous year at the age of thirty-two. A position he was enjoying greatly, especially as there was a cottage in Greenbank to go with the job. Having been summoned by his boss the Laird to discuss future plans for the farm, he stood waiting in the drawing room looking out across the Voe. He spotted Barbara carrying peats from the stack at the bottom of the yard and was thinking back to last year's harvest dance when he had spoken with her brother Magnie, who was obviously trying to get them together. Charles jumped as the Laird entered and stood beside him looking out the window.

"Bonny lass Charles, getting on in years now though. Must be in her mid-thirties I guess. Would make a fine wife. It must be seven or eight years since her intended disappeared to the whaling. We won't see him again, even if he is still alive."

The Laird said nothing for a couple of minutes: "I might be able to consider an increase in wage if we had more sheep. I warrant you could afford to keep a wife, Charles. if you had more income... plenty room for a family in that house at Greenbank."

Rain clouds rolled across Gloup Voe and the drawing room became ominously dark as Charles turned towards John Lawson, unsure what to say.

"Come sit down man", the Laird said. "I think I might have a plan that will suit us both."

****

It was Sunday afternoon and Barbara was sitting at home in front of a glowing peat fire, darning socks, although it was supposed to be a day off. Her mother was working at the Haa and Sam, her father, hadn't been seen for a couple of days, but that was not unusual nowadays as the drinking had become more frequent and it could be a long while before he appeared back. A knock came on the door. Startled, Barbara jumped to her feet. No-one knocked on doors in Yell. Barbara carefully tiptoed to the window with wool and socks held tightly in her arms, and peered out. She couldn't see much beyond the wood replacing broken glass on almost half the window and rain streaming down the two remaining panes. It was most unusual to have a visitor, especially ones that knock. She set down her scurtfull and worryingly made her way towards the door. Lifting the latch the old wooden door creaked as she squinted out to see a large hooded figure outlined against the grey sky and stood back with a start. "Oh my God, Charles..., what..., how..., I mean, can I help?"

"Sorry to gluff de lass. Can I come in?"

"Oh, yes, sorry. Du's weet. Come in, come oot o' da rain. Du's a long way fae hom, is du looking for da Lairds sheep?"

"Can I tak my coat off? Its soaking," he said unbuckling the belt and hanging his dripping jacket on the back of a wooden chair in front of the fire. "Na Babs, I cam to see dee..."

"Oh.... Sit you doon a meenit den an I'll mak a pot o tae."

"Aye dat wid be fine."

Charles sat in silence as Babs took a tin out of the press and spooned some tealeaves into a pot, poured hot water from the kettle that always hung over the fire, and let the brew stew for a short while. "I hope du disna want sugar. Dirs no been any in da hoose for months".

"Naa, I'm fine Babs."

She poured out two mugs and sat down on the opposite side of the table. "Well, I think this will be da first time du's been in dis hoose Charles. We don't get many visitors up here in Vigon. Whit can I do for dee?"

"I'm no' sure whar tae start. Please don't tak dis da wrong way...weel I was windering if du wid like tae come tae da harvest home supper wae me? We could mibbe dance."

Taken aback, Barbara just sat looking at Charles for a minute before diverting her eyes out the window. The rain had stopped and she could see aunt Jessie doing something with the hens across the yard. She had obviously seen the visitor arrive. Barbara's mind wandered back to the last time a man had visited Vigon, Jessie was also tending the hens on that occasion. James was in her thoughts most every day, but one letter was all she had ever received, then nothing. Robbie had found out he had left the whaling and joined a cargo boat, however nothing had been heard from him for over seven years. Barbara turned around to the sound of a pot boiling over.
"Damn...oops sorry Charles. Du's surprised me. Excuse me while I sort oot dis pot. Seriously though, du wants me to be dy partner at da dance?"

"Aye, I ken dis will be a bit o a surprise and I apologise if du disna want to but I'm no' sure when I might manage to speak wi dee afore den. I'm tinkin du'll be working for da Laird again at the supper dis year, but I can wait til later on, when du is free tae dance."

"Weel Charles…" Barbara started to look for an excuse. She didn't want to offend, but his visit and request had been so unexpected she didn't know how to respond.

There was a loud clatter as the outer door opened. Barbara jumped to her feet as Jessie shouted on her way in. "You got the kettle on Babs? She stopped at the inner door wide eyed, looking at the seated figure. "Oh, I didna ken du had a visitor…I'll come back eftir…"

"It's aa right Jessie, come on in. Dis du mind Charles? Aye of course du does. He was just aboot tae ging". Barbara felt her face flush as she stammered to find polite words to explain.

Charles rose from his chair as Jessie watched without saying another word. Barbara picked up his coat and steered him towards the door.

"Thanks for calling Charles. It was kind o de tae stop past. I'll speak anidder day."

Charles stopped before stepping outside, donned the still damp jacket and pulled his hat from the pocket. "Sorry Babs, I'm no very good at dis. Please tink aboot whit I said though. Tanks for da tae." He turned and walked into the rain and didn't look back.

"Well Jessie, don't tell me du wasna aware I hed a veesitor, but tanks. Du couldna hae timed it better!"

Jessie watched Barbara closely as she sat down still a bit flushed. "Aye Babs, I've aye been good at looking oot for abody else. Dat's why I'm still single. So whit wis yon Charlie Russland efter?

****

Eighteen months later the community had become used to seeing Barbara and Charles together. They had been watched by everyone leaving the harvest home dance and local gossip already had them coupled up. "It's was ething dat should have happened years ago" Jessie was telling customers in the Cullivoe shop. "She's been hanging on too long waiting for yon James. Dis applies to all you youngsters," she said turning to address three young lads and a much younger lass sitting inside the shop door waiting politely for Jessie to depart before making their purchases. "Take advantage when you can. We hae a hard life here in the north. Don't be like me and waste your days waiting for better things to turn up".

"Aye, even if something does turn up eventually, by the time you get to Jessie's age you'll be forgotten what to do with it. Ha Ha Ha!" Happy Harry always had the last word.

"Och Jessie, I'm not so sure", Merran said as they walked back along the cart track towards Gloup. "He's probably all right, but I joost hae a feeling he might no be fully committed. He seems ower friendly wi da Laird and I see dem sharing a braw few drams together some nights. Charles certainly will no be paying for dat, so I winder whit John Lawson is up tae. Never any good I doot! But aye, wir Babs seems to hae some of her owld spark back again dis while, so maybe it's for da better".

"Let da lass alone Merran. She needs company and she has a good heed on her. She'll do fine. She's getting on in years though…"

They trudged on quietly, carrying a basket of shopping between them, lost in their own thoughts. "By the way, how's dat guk of a brother of mine dis while? I havna seen him for long, tank God. It is a huge burden for dee and Babs having a selfish owld bastard like dat aroond da hoose, aroond your neck. No winder Magnie never comes hame…"

"Hang on Jessie, I don't want tae fall out. Let's no bring Magnie into dis…he haes enough on his plate keeping his own bairns fed."

"Of coorse Merran, sorry, but I do worry. Du's family and very dear tae me. I am concerned aboot you all and am embarrassed tae admit Sam is a Broon. Mind on, if he ever lifts his hand to de again du must come to me. He widna dare come near his sister.

"Thanks Jessie, dat means a lot and dy support is aye appreciated. I'm sure tings will improve when da summer wadder comes. I dinna worry as much aboot my own problems, it's da bairns. I just hoop Babs kens whit she is getting hersel into…an du's right. Magnie and da family are a worry. My owld midders favourite saying aye comes tae mind: "Peerie bairns, peerie worries… big bairns, big worries."

Ten.

The cargo boat departed Leith with five passengers, including James, standing beside the helmsman. "Be prepared for a bit of a dirl", he said as the crew began to hoist sail. "There's a big black sky up there to the north. Looks like wind on its way, so it might be a good idea to find yourselves a bunk".

James held on to the aft rail with both hands, watching the lights of Edinburgh disappear rapidly behind, feeling a gentle lift of the deck under his feet as the boat rose in the swell. There was an uneasiness in his stomach, not unlike he had felt leaving Shetland all those years ago and heading into the unknown. It was a strange feeling to be coming home after ten years away, knowing things will have changed. It was a very different kind of unknown he was heading towards this time.

"James Sinclair, is that you?" said a gravelly voice behind him.

"Wha's askin?" James said as he turned. In the darkness it wasn't easy to see who was speaking.

"Weel weel", the voice carried on "I towt I saa de come on board at Leith. Boy du's grown up a bit since I last saw de. It was yon whiskers dat had me look twice... du'll be maakin' for hame?"

James looked at the approaching figure for a few awkward seconds before he matched the slightly familiar voice to the face. However it was a much thinner and younger looking person than he'd remembered. "Twenty Quest... Sorry, I mean Tony, Tony Hendry? It can't be, I'm confused."

"Dinna be sorry James, du's nearly right...Tony was my faeder, 'Twenty Questions' was whit dey called him, and aye, everyeen says I'm the spit of my faeder. I'm Tony as well, if du mindes. Am blyde tae see de again."

James shook the offered hand. "Of coorse I mind de, Tony, sorry. It didn'a click right away. Du's caught me be surprise. da last I sa dee was a while back, in Yell."

"Aye, ten, twal years or more I'm tinkin' James. Der's muckle geen on since den. Wir baith gotten mair worry lines an I seem to hae mislaid most o my hair. I moved to Edinburgh in seventeen and faeder died up here twa month ago."

"Oh min, I'm sorry. I didna ken aboot your faeder. He wis a fine man and will be sorely missed. I'm no been back since I left ten year ago, so I hae a dose o' catching up to do. Wis dy faeder been ill?"

Tony cleared his throat, "No. He wis oot gadderin tang i da ebb tae spread apo da land and dey fan him dere when da owld horse kam home alone. He was seventy; dir wis only sixteen years atween us, so we were mair like bridders when I was growing up. Yes he's sorely missed. We are hoping to persuade midder tae come back sooth wae wis and bide. Dere's nothing for her noo in Yell. Portobello is a fine quiet place but she's never been sooth o Lerwick so we'll likely struggle tae tize her".

"Dat's very sad Tony. Please tell di midder I was asking for her. When du's trying to tize her ta shift du should tell da story Happy Harry used to tell about Jeannie and Maggie".

"What story was that?"

"Du's bound to have heard him deliver dis een in his quiet wye, lickly as he poured oot a dram eftir da shop closed".

> "*Jeannie and Maggie were spinsters who lived very fruegally on a small croft in Northmavine. Dey were very reclusive and hardly ever geed oot by da march fence; neither of them had ever been sooth o' da village o' Brae. Da locals towt dem a peerie bit odd but left dem alane. Dey had six (mibbie mair) cats dat were never let oot, so da peerie hoose must have had a rare smell o' its own.*

Not dat I ken dat tae be true...I was never axed in..."

"Ha Ha Ha....."

"Onyway, wan day Maggie cam doon wi a cough an a rash. She felt braally poorly an efter a week sho wis getting worried aboot hersel. A neebor advised her der wis new pheesic in Scalloway, a new fangled potion dat wid cure almost everything. So bravely, Maggie decided to ging dere on her ane.

Da bright lights o' da village wis a huge eye opener for da quiet living spinster. She bade ten days in a room an attended da chemist every day, being eyed closely for any reaction to da pheesic. She wis getting on grand wi da treatment an making good progress, so feeling more energised dan ever Maggie decided to bide a while longer an see whit life was like in dis new found land.

Months geed by an Jeannie back hame in Northmavine wis growin worried. Maggie wis still no back fae da deep sooth, so she was on her own and didna ken whit to do.

Hoosomever, wan day a letter cam fae Maggie. Jeannie sat doon and opened da letter:

> "My Dear Jeannie,
>
> I hope du's weel.
>
> I am ower my illness, tanks to da fine potions I got here in Scalloway from a very nice man.
>
> The world out here is…. weel it's no all bad.
>
> I'll no be comin home… come an join me!
>
> Love,   Maggie x
>
> Ps.   LET DA CATS OOT JEANNIE"

"Ha Ha Ha Ha………."

"His voice was gentle, but du could hear Happy Harry's laugh a mile away wance he had telt wan o' his stories. My version of dis tale is no half da length Harry wid hae streched it, We never kent if dey were true and he never wanted to offend but dey were probably based on some truth. Wan of life's characters is Happy Harry. I look forward tae walking into da Cullivoe shop when I get hame."

Tony was still laughing as they decended the stairway into the saloon "Aye James, I will pass dat story on to midder wi dy compliments."

The journey north was long and very rough as the north of Scotland seas often could be. Passengers were confined below decks during some seemingly impossible acrobatics the boat performed while the gale lasted two days. James felt very frustrated not being able to help. On the morning of day three the weather improved and they passed Fair Isle under full sail with everyone out enjoying the fresh air. "Oh Man dat's a bonny sight", James said to no-one in particular as they approached Sumburgh Head.

The cook came out of his galley door with a full bucket of slops, staggering a bit with the ships movement and stopped alongside James holding on to the rigging to steady himself . "Ah Shetland…high bloody time. Hells own mess down there. Food and puke and god knows what else all over the place." The contents of the bucket disappeared over the side and before it even hit the sea a huge flock of fulmars descended from a previously empty sky and attacked the stinking feast in a feeding frenzy of feathers and noise. Without another word, the cook staggered back into the galley where pots and pans could be heard being thrown around.

"I think you might be wise to move away from the door", said one of the crew as he passed. "Our cook gets a bit high when approaching port…three days without a rum is more than he can manage."

"See them birds?" the crewman said to a small group of passengers, after they had moved forward towards the bow, pointing at the fulmars now gliding alongside waiting for the next scrap to be thrown. "They fly out and meet us at this very same place every time we approach from the south. Always get a feed for their effort. The cook is not as bad as he sounds; well at least with feeding them birds. Clever bird the mallimack."

"Mallimack? Du must be an Orkney man," said James picking up the accent. "In Shetland we call dat bonny big bird a Mallie. But can I tell de something really interesting, withoot trying to soond too much o' a brag. In da Southern Ocean the smaa albatross is called a Mollymawk! Dey look very like yon fulmars we have here, so if dat southern hemisphere bird wasna named by an Orkney sailor I'm a Dutchman..!"

The sea settled down as they sailed north out of the infamous tidal Sumburgh Roost. James was soaking up every detail of his beloved homeland revealing itself in the morning daylight. "What's dat I see up there on the face of the craig? It looks like a lighthouse."

The Orkney crewman took great delight informing James that the lighthouse, a first in Shetland, had been built by the famous Stevenson two years previously.

"This is really good news", said James "Da world is getting busier and shipwrecks around wir coast are far too common. Employers often pit profit afore lives. I'm sure da insurance companies will be in full support as weel, so hopefully everybody wins."

They approached Lerwick in a gentle southerly breeze. James was fully expecting change as the port had been growing rapidly. However ten years had transformed the seafront beyond recognition. Fishing was a huge part of the local economy and the fleet had grown in number and boat size. Ocean going ships from as far afield as Canada were developing new trade routes. It was a busy harbour.

"Du'll be heading north to Yell." James said to Tony as they stood on the foredeck watching the crew manually winch the barque alongside the harbour wall.

"Dis du want tae share a hire across fae Toft? Robbie's cargo boat will be here in a day or twa, but it will likely be a week afore dey get back up to Yell. I'll go see old Davo in the morning, see if he's got a horse and trap to spare tae tak wis up tae Toft. Da peerie ferry boat should be running across Yell Sound noo yon wadder has settled doon. "

As much as James wanted to catch up with Robbie the draw of home was greater. " Fine Tony, lets heed on up north."

Eleven.

It was to be a small reception, with just nearest family and a few friends and neighbours. Sam had been brewing ale for weeks and the ladies were having a day of baking and preparations at Vigon. The evening before a wedding was traditionally a gathering when some ale would be sampled and a fiddle or two would appear in the brides house. This was called the contract night.

Merran was having to work at the Haa into the afternoon so Jessie was in charge until she could join them after her shift. Merran was still having reservations about Babs and Charles, but had made herself promise to help ensure all went well for the big day.

Merran was just about to descend the stairs when the front door of the Haa burst open and John Lawson entered. She stopped, looking down from the upper landing to see his bedraggled state and a mood to match. She slunk back into the darkness.
"Elizabeth.... you there?"

"John, what in Gods name are you shouting about? What's wrong?"

"Bad news. I've just been to Cullivoe, the bloody gossip…"

"Shush man, keep your voice down… walls have ears. Take your boots off and come through to the drawing room."

Elizabeth shut the heavy oak door behind him with a thunk as he strode across the room and poured a large brandy. She waited for her husband to speak, knowing that to prompt him would be a wrong move at this point.

"It's that bloody James Sinclair. Harry in the shop told me the man was seen yesterday in Ulsta."

"Well I'm sure that has little to do with you John. Times have moved on. He was Barbara Brown's old boyfriend, that I do know. What might he have done to upset you?"

"Don't you see? He could ruin everything."

"Look John, Barbara and Charles are getting married tomorrow. They are moving to Greenbank as you arranged. Your precous sheep numbers will multiply once you get the grazing around Vigon sorted. Rightly or wrongly John Lawson, you are, as usual, in control."

Merran tiptoed away from the door and into the kitchen when she heard the Laird take a few steps across the floor. She staggered a bit before grabbing a chair beside the now cold stove and sat down. *"Oh God! Dis soonds too much. I need tae speak wi Babs. Charles hasna mibbie been fully honest, or at least he is being used by da Laird for his own ends. And James...James is back!"*

Hearing a faint creaking floorboard in the hall, John Lawson diverted from the drinks cabinet and smartly opened the door, but no-one was there. He closed the door quietly and returned to the brandy decanter. Turning around with the refilled glass in his hand. "Which staff are on duty this evening Elizabeth?"

"I believe Merran will be the only one left. She has two days leave and goes home shortly to prepare for the wedding."

"Merran..., Barbara Brown's mother..."

Merran removed her pinny, dropped it into the laundry basket and turned around. She jumped as the Laird stood in the doorway.

"Ah! Merran, is that you finished for the day?"

"Yes mister Lawson. Da mistress telt me I can ging hom. We hae a big day da morn."

He stood and stared, eyes following the buttons down her blouse. "You'd better get your things from the room and make your way home then I suppose..."

He smirked as she uncomfortably squeezed past.

Merran was now in a bit of a panic and hurriedly climbed the stairs to her attic bedroom and threw a few things into a bag. She turned to see John Lawson watching from the landing. He slowly moved through the doorway, never taking his eyes off her and closed the door behind him.

"Please dinna do onything du might regret, mister Lawson. I can work extra days next week if dat's whit you want mister Lawson…please." She backed into the corner with her bag clutched tightly to her chest and hunkered down.

John Lawson approached, his pale blue eyes looking down with sheer anger. "You were listening to a private conversation. I will not tolerate that kind of behaviour. You will stay in this room until I return. Be warned. Any attempt to get out will result in some very severe consequences for you and your family. You will be free to go home to your hovel when I return later…not one minute before." He turned, removed the key and closed the door, locking it from the outside.

"What on earth is going on John?" Elizabeth Lawson was standing over her husband as he sat on the doorstep putting his boots on.

"I'm off to see Charles Rusland, I'm not going to let that Sinclair bloke spoil things at this late stage. Don't let that damned woman out of her room until I get back."

"We can't keep her here John, It's kidnap…" Elizabeth shrieked.

"Whisht woman, just a couple of hours. Do not make this any more difficult. A lot of money hinges on this marriage taking place, you'll see," and he marched off towards the stables.

Everything had gone quiet in the house as Merran tried to pull the door open. She pushed and kicked, but it was solid. She had no idea of what was happening downstairs and making a noise might not be a good idea. *"Hell dis is a mess. I need to speak wi Babs…urgently."*

The bedroom was three storeys up in the big house with one tiny window in the gable end, too high to jump from. Ever resourceful though, Merran began tying sheets together. There was no shortage of linen as the attic rooms of the big house were very cold, and she had gathered a number of old sheets over the winter to keep warm. She tied the first sheet to the old iron bed and fed the rest out the window. Visibly shaking with anger fright and worry, she quietly edged the bed across the room towards the window, clambered up and scrambled her way, feet first onto the deep ledge and began to wriggle through the tiny opening. Her skirts getting pushed above her head as she moved, and the wooden window frame dug into her front as she wriggled further and further out. Merran soon realised she was beyond the point of no return. Holding tight onto the knotted sheet her knuckles scored the stone cill, but she was outside and vertical, lowering herself hand over hand down the rough stone gable of the Haa.

It was a very painful long walk home to Vigon. She had stopped a number of times to bathe her cuts and bruises in the watery peat banks and to think. "*It might not be good at this time to tell everyone what had been overheard. James would be in the vicinity, so maybe play things down initially to see what happens next*". As she walked into the house they stopped and looked. "Oh! Merran, what on earth has happened? Dy claes are all torn and bloody.... is that blood Merran?"

"It's my own fault" said Merran as she sat in front of the fire with a mug of warm milk in her hands and everyone fussing around. "I towt I wid tak a shortcut across da Mares Pool and slipped, joost in too big a hurry to get hom and help. Stop da worry and get back to your baking lasses."

They all laughed at the situations Merran constantly got herself into and went back to the food preperations. Jessie sidled up to Barbara and said quietly "Shortcut be damned.... I don't believe dat. Du hae a word wae her Babs. She'll tell dee... get da real story."

An hour later Barbara and Merran slipped through to the ben end of the house,"Well midder, lets have it."

"Dis is going to soond unreal Babs. Listen to da end.... I want de tae mak up dy own mind whit tae mak o it."

When her mum had finished Barbara stood up, tears streaming down. "Dis du ken whit? Du's a special mam and have aye been my saviour on so many occasions. Whit du's done dis day is something no many wid have, or could have done. Thanks mam. Hell I'm frightened though for whit da Laird might be up to."

"Babs, dinna worry. Da Laird dusna bother me. Everybody says dir's mair in his sheeks dan in his breex."

"Midder!"

"Sorry Babs" Merran said with a hint of a smile. "I need to tell de though, an was going to say dis after the wedding. I'm going back to Fetlar. Dy faeder an me wid be better off apart. Dis is da end of me working at da Haa noo ony wye, so I hae nothing tae lose. I should hae gone years ago…"

"Oh midder, dis is crazy. I'm no sure noo aboot Charles's motives. I tink I still love James but I don't ken if he still has feelings for me. Whit can I do?"

"All right Babs, I doot dat if James has any respect left, and some care for de after all dese years, he might make an appearance here afore da day is oot. Not that I ken he will turn up, it's joost dy midders witchey ways and a bit o hope thrown in! Du needs to hae a big think. Go an hide in dy special place and wait. I'll tell him whar to fin de if he turns up here. If he disna appear it might help de mak dy decision".

"My special place. Hoo dis du ken aboot my special place?"

"Goodness bairn, whit kind o a midder dis du tink I am if I didna ken aboot dat? Dinna worry, I'm pretty sure naebody else kens though."

Barbara wrapped a big coat around her shoulders and slipped out the door.

Merran rejoined the noisy gathering in the kitchen, announcing she was feeling much better and had advised Babs to have a lie-down before her big day tomorrow.

Twelve.

James paused outside the Cullivoe shop with his hand on the door latch. It was more than ten years since he last stood here. Much would have changed, not least himself, but the familiarity of home was comforting. There was a loud ping as he opened the door. "Bloody hell Harry, that gave me a gluff. What's wi da bell?"

"Praise be to aald Nick, it's James! Come on in young man. Joost look at da sight afore me. All grown up! Welcome home. It's been a while, du must hae made dy fortune by noo."

"Harry, it's fine tae see dee again. And du's looking good man. I hop all is fine wae dee. I'm no bidin long, but I will be back for a yarn, an tae share a brew. Am needing a peerie bit o help."

"Weel du kens me James boy, aye been here to help. Whit can I do for de?"

"I'm hearing dat Babs is getting married da morn. I need to go up to Vigon and wish her weel afore I ging onywye else. She'll be dere making preparations. Could du do me a favour and store my gear til I win back?"

"Ah min, of coorse. Dat will be no bodder, joost dump it roond da back... this way."

"Du's a gem Harry. Sorry no to be bidin langer. It's a bit rude but du kens da wye. I didna manage tae take home a whale steak but I hae a peerie faering fae da southern ocean dat I will look oot for de when I get back."

James gave a smirk expecting a cheeky response followed by the traditional big laugh. However Harry sidled up quietly. "Da Laird was here no an hoor past, axin aboot de James. Second time the day. He seems to ken do is back. I'm no sure whit he is up to, but I don't trust him. Go canny. Steer weel clear o da Haa as du passes through Gloup."

James thanked Harry with promises to return for his possessions the next day and set off westwards. *"Da laird axin questions was not good news. I tink I might tak Harry's advice an follow da sheep track avoiding Gloup an Westafirth."*

Unaccustomed to walking so far over hills and heather, James arrived exhausted and sat himself down on a familiar stone wall. The late afternoon sun was beginning to settle into the north west and there was noise and hilarity coming from inside. "Messed it up James boy..., bloody messed it up. What da hell am I doing here?" James said aloud as he stood up and stared across the kale yard.

"James Sinclair! God Almighty du's back!"

James swung around so fast he stumbled against the wall. "Merran, whit da hell? Whit's du doing oot here?" Seeing her stand up on the other side of the wall and smooth her skirt down he realised what she had been doing in the kale yard. "Sorry, Merran, I hope I didna disturb dee. I mean, am so blyde tae see dee Merran. Sorry. Is Babs here?"

"Oh James, is dis really dee? My God man it is so good to see dee here. Come gie me a bosie." she leaned over the wall and wrapped her arms tightly around him.

Merran had never so much as touched him before, so this was most unexpected and a bit embarrasing. She let go and just stood looking. "Is Babs in da hoose Merran? I need tae speak…, congratulate her."

"I dinna ken where tae begin James." Merran said as she took a step back. "Min, du's been away a long time. No Babs is not at da hoose."

"Oh Merran, I've mucked things up…"

"Aye James, I heard de say dat a meenit ago indeed. I don't hae time tae listen to dy tales ee noo, but I do tink Babs needs dee. Ten years is a long while, but for some reason she still loves de, James. She is waiting in the cave, du kens whar to ging. Tings hae gone in a witter. I sent her to your special place no twa hours ago. I joost kent du wid turn up dis evening. I just kent du wid."

"Merran…"

"No James, just ging. Babs will explain everything." She turned and strode back up to Vigon without looking back.

"*Compose dysel James.*" He stood still a few short minutes, took a deep breath and turned west across the park towards the headland in a daze. With heart pounding loudly, he descended the familiar route towards the craigs. James was very nervous. "*Merran obviously kens aboot da cave. Babs is waiting there…ten years on! Hoo is dis going to pan oot. Can I ever explain? "Tings have gone in a witter" Merran said… Whit does dat all mean….?*"

James came to the steepest part and scrambled down. A scarfie (or cormorant as he had discovered was the real name in a book), plunged into the surf below as he approached. Slithering along the cliff edge as he and Barbara had done many times before hand in hand. A few stones disloged as he descended.

All was quiet, edging his way along the narrow ledge and holding his breath. Unsure. Doubts multiplying. He hesitated. What right did he have to be here? Things had changed; Shetland had changed, he himself was not the same young lad that left these shores so long ago. "*All grown up James*" Tony

Hendry had said. What will Babs be like now? He stopped and looked. A familiar heart-shaped stone was propped up near the entrance. She was indeed here alone. Instinctively ducking his head he stepped into the dark interior.

"James, du cam back. It is dee James, it really is…"

"Babs…..dis is unreal. Where can I begin. Hoo can I even start tae explain….."

"No yet James. There will be plenty o' time for words, joost hold me." They stood for a long while tightly wrapped together. "I have missed de so very much."

James's voice was full of emotion as he whispered quietly, "Babs, I too have yearned. For ten years I have missed dy sweet voice. Will du marry me?"

Barbara gave a shriek and stood back. "James, dis du ken nothing?"

"I tink dat will probably be fairly accurate, so tell me Babs".

"All right James, a very short version to begin and don't interupt".

Half an hour later Babs stopped. "Noo afore du says onything my answer is YES. I really really really wid like dat, but as I just telt de da morm is my wedding day!"

"Oh! Babs, dis is joost crazy. We need to move fast, while dere's still some daylight. Is James Moar at

Westafirth still the Precentor? I will ging ower dere. Wait here, I'll be back in a blink. Trust me Babs, I will make it up, all dose years we've missed, I will make it up. Please wait. But first can I have a smooriken?"

Barbara stood in a daze watching her James once again depart, more confused than ever, "Gang warily James."

Thirteen.

The Contract Feast and party at Vigon continued into the evening with free flowing ale, laughter and music which could be heard a mile away. Every so often someone would venture out and search buildings and sheep punds in the area. However popular belief was that Barbara had gone to spend the evening in Cullivoe with Charles, so there was nothing to worry about and the party could continue. Sam picked up the poker, wiped it with a wet cloth and pushed it into the glowing embers of the peat fire. A few minutes later the sparkling hot iron was plunged into his ale jug...

"Pizzed ale," Sam announced " Gods cure for a sore heed an a cowld heart! Drink up everybody, der's plenty mair whar dat cam fae."

Merran stood up and opened the press door."I tink something tae eat wid be an idea Sam. It's going tae be a lang day da morn and du'll no stand the pace at dis rate. I'll get some bannocks on da go."

Sam said nothing, glaring suspiciously through his drawn eyebrow bush at Merran as he noisily supped his warm brew.

"Whit on earth can have happened tae wir lass though?" Jessie said quietly to Merran as they began to clear a space on the table. "Du geed for a piss earlier and den Babs geed ben…. bit she's no dere noo."

Merran sat down again and whispered "I'll tell dee later Jessie. I need to ging oot an errand. Keep things going here." She needed to find out what was happening with James and Babs, and donning a coat she slipped out once again. Taking a long diversion south before turning towards the cliffs, along the south burn of Vigon there was a hooded figure in the distance, also making way towards the cliffs. Although it was now getting dark it looked like James. She ducked down not wanting to be seen stalking. She wondered for a short while and second guessing, turned back and traced the route he might have taken towards Westafirth.

A couple of hours later Merran arrived back home and went directly to the ben end of Vigon. There were still some voices and a fiddle through the other end of the house, so all seemed good so far. She was packing clothes into a bag when Jessie walked in. "Merran, whit….?"

"Shush Jessie, dey'll hear dee. It's time I let de ken. Sit doon. I need help and Jessie, keep dis quiet for noo. I'll begin wi whit happened tae me doon at da Haa."

When Merran had finished, albeit a very brief version, Jessie stood up with her mouth wide open. "Oh! Merran, du could have died escaping fae dat big hoose. What wis he going to do wae de when he cam back? And them bairns, Merran, hidden awa in yon owld cave. Da Laird is unpredictible. Whit might he do if he finds them? Whit can we do?"

"Stay calm Jessie and gie nothing away. He will never fin dem. We need to keep everybody through da hoose happy for a while yet. Dere's a bottle o whisky in da back o da press… pour some oot tae da men, an just mak sure dey don't mak for home yet. I will run across to Babs and James in the morning wi some claes and maet. Dey might need tae disappear for a blink".

"Of course I will lass. Get what du needs done and I will keep da smoke and mirrors going."

"Whit is du speakin' aboot? Smoke an Mirrors? Dere's mair tae dee dan meets da eye Jessie Broon! Tanks though. I can guess at whit du means. My God, I don't tink da morn will be like any we've seen afore. As weel, it might be wise for me tae keep well oot o da Lairds rodd. He'll most certianly blame me for everything an come looking."

"Tak care lass, tak care. Jessie rose to her feet and opened the ben door. Men be damned, I'll be pooring a dram for da weemin as weel." She strode back through to the party slamming the outside door as she went past and pulling at her skirts to make it look like she had returned from toileting. " Come on den aabody, drink up. Here's to Bab's big day da morn... wha wants a drop o whisky?"

****

Despite being wrapped together all night, the unlikely runaways were cold. James swung damp legs over the rock plinth and stood up blowing into his hands and beating flux. "Right Babs, we need tae get goin. James Moar is a good man. He promised last night tae support an help wis. As lippened by law I lodged a line for the Pawns an paid wir fee for da calling o da Banns. He'll proclaim in da kirk dis morning early. Is du sure du wants to ging through wi dis?"

"For the hundredth time James of coorse I do. I made a queek decision to be here for de James. I ken it wis da right een. I do love dee so much…but my god, whit have we done? Aabody oot dare will be windering whit has happened. I hoop dey dinna tink I'm geen ower da kraeg. Dis is my wedding day. Oh! James… "

"I love dee as weel Babs. My god though, dy mam… she steered us tagidder an we will lickly need her help again afore dis all comes to a heed. A wonderful wife is Merran. Lets get moving. It's a fair hike tae Cullivoe."

James rapped on the manse door a second time before it opened. Reverend Charles Cowan initially appeared non too pleased to be disturbed so early, but invited the wet and untidy couple into his house. "I apologise for the intrusion at such an early hour but can du, as a man of God, please find it in dy heart to hear wis oot? Du'll mind my family, the Sinclairs. I am James and have been awa for a number of years. I am no a religious man but I do however respect dy standing within da community and am aware du is a good man, personally supporting many families through difficult times. We need dy support and a kind heart to help wis oot."

The bedraggled pair related a condensed verson of their ten year separation and of why they wished to now get married in such haste. "Well, you put me in a bit of a predicament. Most unusual…, the Banns for the marriage of you Barbara and Charles Rusland are in my diary to be read today at noon. The marriage is then scheduled to take place at six o'clock, as you are obviously aware. However you tell me the Precentor has also been paid for Banns to be read for yourself and James Sinclair, which may have already been read out in the church this morning. Well Barbara, your mother and I go back a long way and you have convinced me she fully supports this action. I see no legal reason why this cannot happen. Now come through to the kitchen where my wife will give you a bite to eat and make you more presentable to enter the house of God."

Babs and James looked at each other quite taken aback. "This is very kind," James said to the minister. "We will never be able to thank you enough. I hope we aren't making things difficult. We are so grateful."

"You are welcome and I am happy to help. However I am aware this will create some local upset. Might it be an idea to take yourselves away for a few days after the ceremony?"

The lovers removed wet outer garments and were led through into the warm kitchen. At about midday they walked across to the Cullivoe kirk where the minister asked for the Banns to again be called three times. Once the congregation were seated he delivered a shortened version of his normal Sunday sermon and concluded with the marriage of Barbara and James to a rather stunned gathering of worshippers.

They were both light headed with the whole situation and unsure what would happen next. The Reverend Cowan led them to the back vestray and as they began to deliver thanks he held up his hand. "Shush, there's no time to waste. There are men on horses outside who are unaware of what has just taken place in the church, but who will no doubt very soon learn. So keep your heads low, go out the back door and make haste across the hill. I will distract them around the front as the congregation leave. God bless and may he keep you safe."

It was a much longer route back. They had avoided being seen initially by crawling behind the sheep dyke and heading up past Kussa Waters. However the most worrying couple of minutes had been overhearing the laird on horseback outside the kirk, mustering recruits to begin a search. He was decisive, very influential and was obviously aware both James and Barbara were missing. He would soon discover the marriage had taken place under his nose and things could get very difficult.

Back at the cave a couple of large canvas bags were tucked inside the entrance and a small flat stone with a scratched X lay on top. "Oh midder, du is a saviour."

They donned dry clothing and despite the bread and cheese received from the ministers wife, both were still fantin. They sat down together on the rocky floor and opened the bag of food.

"James, dis is unreal. It feels like a dream. Da minister dis morning; can du believe whit he did for wis? Mam is somehow ahint all dis, but how…? You…me…married. I still can't believe it. We hae a lot o catching up to do an assuming da Laird doesna come chapping at da door, we will hae a few days tae do just dat. Mr and Mrs. St Clair, I like da soond of dat."

"Weel Babs, I tink da Saint bit might be a bit far fetched, an definitely mair as da minister could endow upo wis, but I can get used wi Mr and Mrs."

"Och James, I wis maakin fun." Barbara laughed. "Seriously though, when I was doon apon tings an tinkin' I wid never see de again, my midder was a huge support and she tried tae steer me in da right direction. She wad say *"Better loose dan ill teddered Babs."* Well as du kens I didna pay ony attention, and wis so nearly ill teddered."

They sat a few minutes listening to the hush of the sea and the birds outside. James picked up Barbaras cold hands. "Da many times du… we, stayed here in dis cave seems a lifetime ago. Well, tanks tae me it's been far too mony years. We towt it wis wir secret place, dat naebody in da world knew. We were young and towt we had invented love. Looking back hoo did we get awa wi it? My god we were naive Babs.… Dy midder is a wise old burd. She obviously kent what wis happening and here she is again, supporting her peerie bairn. I'm still no sure hoo this will end, but she has browt wis tagedder again, and has gaen wis a breathing space. We need tae tak advantage and mak plans.… hopefully da right eens!"

Fourteen.

The bones of a plan was hatched and as soon as daylight arrived on day four they began their trek south.
Thankfully there was not much to carry other than some food which would make the hike easier.

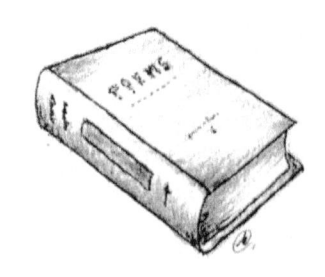

Going away, leaving Yell was an obvious goal. However the ferry boat called past infrequently and the Laird would probably have the three piers watched. Ulsta was over sixteen miles away, Mid Yell eight and Gutcher five, but that was as the crow flies, so keeping to well trodden paths avoiding lochs and peat bogs they would have to walk many more miles. They had agreed on Glippapund as a first stop as it was only a couple of miles away and somewhere they guessed the Laird would not initially be looking. Glippapund was remote even by Shetland standards, and Bessie was a fine soul and somehow always up with the latest gossip.

The morning was fine and after taking some additional diversions from the normal route, they arrived at the tiny house which doubled up as a shop and post office. "Babs, it's dee. Is du no the speak o' da parish," was the greeting as they opened the door. "And my whit a fine lad du has turned oot tae be master James Sinclair."

"Well, that wasna as bad a greeting as I lippened Bessie. If du has a minute to spare can we bide for a blink?"

"Du kens fine Babs, du is aye welcome here whenever. Bit whit an onkerry du has stirred up. Yon Laird has gone by his mind. Du got married. Weel done lass. It gets a bit longersome up here on me own an du is just da tonic I am needing. Come troo da back an tell me all aboot it."

They were treated like royalty and in exchange for James taking a few loads of peat from the hill while the women yarned, they were invited to stay for a reested mutton supper and a bed for the night.

Next morning was back to dreech low cloud and drizzle which engulfed the hillside. With hats pulled down and collars turned up they trudged on for a mile or so before speaking. "I tink we need tae try an get tae Mid Yell Babs. A boat fae dere tae Lerwick would be whit we want. I could maybe catch up wi owld Robbie Nisbet and see if yon business deal is still on offer. He'll certainly look eftir wis."

"I am worried about mam James. Leaving her back dere on her own."

" Lets stop a blink and rest Babs. Dere's a lee spot here aside da ditch." James wrapped his arm around Barbara and pulled his heavy coat above their heads as they sat hunched up, backs to the drizzle. "She has

Jessie, dy faither an lots o idder support fae friends. She's no bad at looking eftir hersel either."

"Me faeder is worthless. He's no done any work on the croft for years. He's a lazy drunken buggar. If it wasna for Jessie and mam Vigon wid hae disappeared long ago. He's no short o liftin his hand when he's minded an I ken she has spoken aboot leaving, going back hom tae Fetlar. Mibbie noo dat I hae made a break it could be da turning point…"

"Oh Babs, I'm so sorry. I have caused de such grief. I will support whitever du wants tae do."

Tears were now rolling down her cheeks. "No, of course du's no James. Da problems are been dere for years, so maybe just da opposite noo it's all oot in da open. Me leaving might joost be whit was needed. Midder hates working at da Haa and only does it tae keep maet on da teeble. Mr Lawson has lickly figured oot she was helping me tae avoid dis whit I noo see as a contrived marriage tae his stockman Charles Russland. So I guess she'll no be going back dere tae work. Midder might be da wan needin support noo though. I don't think I can leave Yell, no yet, no kenan mam is still dere amang it all. I tink da village at Mid Yell might joost be too busy for wis tae slip trow athoot bein seen onywye."

"All right Babs, lets move on. I ken someen wha might help. Hit's a fair bit tae ging yet and am drookled, da rain is seepin right throw tae my…"

"James!"

They grinned at each other and stood up. Walking silently hand in hand for a couple of hours their spirits brightened as the weather faired up.

"Du kens Babs, da Southern Ocean seas were big. I cannot deny dere wis times when I was worried, even a bit gluffed. We sometimes sailed on wan tack for weeks on end, and dat could be brally langersome. I wis sad, I wis lonely an sometimes never spoke a word for days. I towt aboot hame and towt aboot dee aften. Wan night da wind eased an we were gently gliding alang wi softly creaking rigging and waves whispering past. I was leaning on da bow quarter watching da stars abeun looking for da Southern Cross, when old Scrubber, Scrubber Scott stopped by my side.

"Fine night James." he said. Weel Scrubber said "fine night" every night, but on dis occasion he wis actually no far wrong!

"Aye, fine night Scrubber," I answered athoot turnin aroond.

"Have you heard of Charles Gray in your travels James?"

"Can't say I have", I responded."

"He's in the Royal Marines. Published a volume of poetry a few years back...hailed from the Scottish town of Anstruther no less. Near where I live."

"Am never heard o him Scrubber. "I assume dis is gan tae lead somewye", I replied, no really interested."

"Well listen you here James. This is my favourite poem." An he spak fae da heart wi dis lovely words...

Grim Winter Was Howlin'

Grim winter was howlin' owre muir and owre mountain
  And bleak blew the wind on the wild stormy sea:
The cauld frost had lock'd up each riv'let and fountain,
  As I took the dreich road that leads north to Dundee.

  Though a'round was dreary, my heart was fu'cheerie.
  And cantie I sung as the bird on the tree;
For when the heart's light, the feet winna soon weary,
  Though ane should gang further than bonnie Dundee!

Arrived at the banks o' sweet Tay's flowin river,

*I look'd, as it rapidly row'd to the
sea;*
And fancy, whose fond dream still
pleases me ever,
　Beguiled the lone passage to
bonnie Dundee.

There, glowrin' about, I saw in his
station
　Ilk bodie as eydent as midsummer
bee;
When fair stood a mark, on the face
o' creation,
　The lovely young Peggy, the pride
o' Dundee!

O! aye since the time I first saw this
sweet lassie,
　I'm listless, I'm restless, wherever
I be:
I'm dowie, and donnart and aften
ca'd saucy;
　They kenna it's a'for the lass o'
Dundee!

O! lang may her guardians be virtue
and honour;
　Though anither may wed her, yet
well may she be;
And blessin's in plenty be shower'd
down upon her –
　The lovely young Peggy, the pride
o' Dundee!"

"Oh James, dat's a lovely poem! Du is such a romantic. I hoop dere's anidder een whar dat cam fae."

"Da words o' idders Babs. I wish I had da abeelity to have written it. Tanks tae aald Scrubber though, for makin me feel good again when I wis brally low. I towt aboot dee every time I sang it."

"Du sang it! Is it a song?"

"Weel no really, but I set it tae a tune o my own as dat wis da only way I could mind da words. Ah!…look up there aheed lass. Dat big hose on da brae. Lets get wirsels ap dere afore da mirknen."

Fifteen

The door was opened by a man, similar in height, but a bit more stocky than James, although standing two steps up he towered above them. He looked down, first at James then Barbara, his head tilted slightly, like a dog waiting for instruction.

"Sorry. Wasn't expecting visitors."

"Sorry. I wisna expectin tae be passin," came James's reply.

Barbara looked at James, then back at the man in the door, not knowing what to think...

"My God, it's James. What the hell? It is you isn't it? Yon beard man. You look older."

"Aye, Malcolm, aboot ten years older dan da last time we met," said James with a grin, "I've been away since '13. Is du still rustling a few sheep ta mak ends meet?"

Barbara took a step back, thinking James was spoiling for a fight...

"Now this is a surprise, and not an unpleasant one." His accent had a bit of an English twang. "Come in, come in James man and introduce me to this lovely lass."

They were led through the hall and into what was probably the drawing room, basically but tastefully furnished. However it was cold, felt unused and unlived in. "Sit you down. I'll go fetch Olivia and the kids. How are you doing James? This is amaizing. Sorry, I'll just be back."

Barbara sat looking around "Dis is mighty grand James, how dis du ken him? Windhoos is da Lairds hoose. He owns a lot o land aroond Lumbister. I've heard of him bit never met. Dis is a bit daunting…"

"Don't fret lass, Malcolm is wan o da best, believe me. He looks a bit o a neep, but we were were pals years back. We owe each other a few favours."

Two tiny figures entered the room and stood looking at the unexpected guests. Silent. The girls could not have been much more than five years old, with curling blond hair and dressed in light blue frilly frocks. They just stood and said nothing.

James ventured to make conversation. "Ah, you must be Jack and Jill. Have you been up the hill for a pail o' water?"

No answer.

"Malcolm appeared at the doorway behind them. "You always took a trick with the bairns James. However, my daughters might present a challenge. It's their age. We don't get many visitors, and they can be a bit shy, aren't you girls? But if anyone can crack the enamel you will my old pal." I am delighed to introduce my twin daughters Charlotte and Vaila."

The girls were ushered further into the room and sat quietly beside each other on a chaise- lounge under the window.

Turning around he introduced Olivia. "My wife, my inspiration and definitely my saviour. James, my old friend, you will understand where I come from there."

"Malcolm, tank you very much for inviting wis into dy home. It means a lot, and I will let you ken why we have turned up withoot invitation in a start. Da last time we met du wis so full o ale I carried you home...to dis very hoose. Dy aald man was livid. He threatned to hae me shot. A bit scary at da time and no my fault du had scooped mair ale as aabody else. However he did apologise da next morning an tanked me for looking eftir de. Dat wis a lot o years ago."

"Times have moved on James. Sadly, dad died not two years ago and I have taken over the estate. But hey, I'm eager to know, what brings you chapping at Windhouse? And please introduce us to your lady friend."

They yarned late into the night and were plied generously with food and drink. The ladies imediately bonded and found lots in common to chat about as James and Malcolm reminisced in a world of their own. The girls had been encouraged to go to bed early and had given everyone a goodnight kiss. Olivia said she would come and tuck them up an a minute, but Barbara noticed both girls hesitated and without question Olivia took them through and was gone a long while before returning.

****

"Dis du believe in God James?" asked Barbara.

"Mmmm, no sure. I think I wid need tae get some sleep afore dis conversation gings ower deep. Too mony drams in my body."

"James...."

"All right Babs. Depends on what du's going tae say next."

"Well, someen or someting is oot dere looking eftir wis. A week ago I was destined tae get married tae Charles Russland. I hoop du understands James. Du had disappeared fae my life for ten years an he was offering tae gie me a new home an a new begining. I telt de afore dat I noo see I wis being used and probably poor Charles was as weel. I must hiv been blind tae no see dat his boss, da Laird, wis displacing families. Tenant crofters and hooseholds across north Yell are being evicted fae generations o family occupation to introduce mair sheep. Dat's a very lucritive income for da estate I believe, but hugely devastating for wir community. I am so glad du turned up, James. I winder if God sent de tae save me?"

"If God wis a clever god he should be looking at stopping John Lawson in his tracks. Dat wid end da suffering. Poverty, distress and deprivation is happening aroond wis and appears to be increasing, alang wae da Lairds bank balance. So maybe the Devil himsel is oot and aboot. I'm sorry but I don't hae much religion left in me Babs. Aefter some of whit I've witnessed dese past years, I hae reservations. I do though respect dem dat need the comfort o worship. Everybody needs comfort. My aald faedder used to say *"Du's dealt dy cards"*. I don't see God being able to mak da changes we wish for. Hooever let wis hae a good look at da cards we hae been dealt and if we play dem right I believe tagidder we might joost hae a winning hand."

Barbara snuggled up in James's arms: "A roof ower wir heads an a four poster bed. Dis is unexpected luxury. I'm tinkin' du could indeed be right."

Sixteen

Charlotte and Vaila were tucking into bread and honey at the breakfast table as James and Barbara entered the kitchen. "Good morning Mr and Mrs Sinclair, cup of tea?" Olivia asked without turning from stirring a pot on the stove.

"Oh tae widd be lovely Olivia," answered Barbara. "Can I do onything to help?"

"Just sit you down Barbara. Thanks, but we have breakfast under control, don't we girls?"

They nodded heads in tandem.

"Malcolm has gone down to the village to see if the cargo boat is in yet. He should be back shortly, so girls, once we have finished breakfast you have a choice. Dishes need washing or do you want to show Barbara and James around the house?

"We'll show them around", said Vaila.

"Aha! So you do hae a voice" said James. "I'm keen to see whit you can tell me about your lovely home Windhouse."

The girls ate up and politely sat waiting for the others to finish.

James laid his napkin on the table and got to his feet. Excusing himself from the table he took hold of Barbara's hand."Right lasses let the tour begin."

As soon as they stepped outside both girls excitedly began to speak over each other. "Woha slow up lasses, one at a time."

"We are going to Lerwick," Vaila said, "as soon as the boat arrives."

"And we will be going to school", added Charlotte.

"Indeed lasses, your mam was telling wis lastnight you are going to bide dere a while. I love Lerwick." replied Barbara.

They were led around to the back of Windhouse and looking up the hill, Vaila pointed to some ruinus stone work."That's the old house. It wasn't very good, so they knocked it down and built this one down here, nearer the road."

"You are very lucky to live in such a grand house."

"Mummy doesn't like it," said Charlotte. "She says bad things happen here".

"I don't think that can be true" said James as the girls led them further around what once would have been the back garden, but now was just part of the hillside where sheep appeared to have stripped everything bare.

"Oh yes, Daddy told his friends…"

"Told them what?" asked James, concious they may be straying into a subject the girls should not be discussing.

"Well…" Charlotte stopped and pointed up to a window. "See that room there with the curtains drawn? We overheard Daddy tell his friends about one night when there were visitors staying with grandad. As they entered the room the lamp they carried went out, so they lit it again and it went out again. That night they just couldn't get a lamp to stay on in the room, so they slept in another room, the one you are in."

Vaila was eager to speak, "We heard Mummy and Daddy argue. She said the house was bad and other things were happening. She wants to leave…"

Charlotte continued, "We went into that room one night."

"On your own?" asked Barbara.

"Yes."

"What happened?"

"The lamp went out" Vaila butted in. "We screamed and dropped the lamp, we were scared. There's now a big oil stain on the floor and it stinks when you pass, even with the door closed. Charlotte cries in bed every night since then. Mummy says it will be fine in Lerwick though."

The girls changed the subject and moved on with the tour, showing off their play areas. They proved to have a very good local knowlege, pointing out landmarks, explaining how the otters lived and reared offspring as far inland as Windhouse. They pointed out a skylark way above and were able to identify bird song even if they couldn't see them. As they stood admiring the panoramic view, the girls saw their dad striding up towards the house and ran to meet him.

"Noo dat wis a bit o an odd tale" Barbara said quietly. "It kind o helps explain why da lasses were so quiet at bedtime lastnight. Dis du tink we should say something tae Malcolm and Olivia?"

"Poor bairns. Scary things like dat can hae a lasting effect. I'm no sure whit tae tink. Dey seemed happier wance dey had telt us aboot it Babs. Lets leave weel alone unless Malcolm or Olivia mentions something."

"Good morning you pair. I hope the Bridal Suite was to your liking?"

"Indeed it was Malcolm." James saw Barbara blush a little. "Du had an early start dis morning. Olivia said you were awa doon tae Mid Yell."

"I was looking for old Robbie to take us down to Lerwick. Or from what you told me last night we should maybe call it the Sinclair Nisbet Shipping Company. Ha Ha. All nonsense aside though, as discussed lastnight, Olivia and the kids will be relocating there until we make some decisions about what is going to happen with this place. The boat is apparently due in to Gutcher tomorrow with supplies. John James, the agent said he will get him to stop past Mid Yell to pick us up on the way back. So we have about three days to get ready."

"Dat sounds good Malcolm. I need to speak wi aald Robbie as soon as possible. Recent events have got my brain in a fog, so I need to mak some plans. Tree days is no long for de to get packed up, so hopefully we might be able tae help?"

"That will be really good if you can stop long enough to give us a hand to get everything packed. In fact I feel a plan coming on that might help you out."

Seventeen

Two days later the packing was all but complete and the adults were chatting together over a cup of tea in the kitchen. Malcolm suggested James and he should go a walk to check the sheep and leave the ladies to yarn in peace. It was a pleasant afternoon as they followed a sheep track up the hill, crooks in hand. Malcolm stopped and sat down on a big stone pulling a hip flask from his pocket. "I'm not as fit as I thought I was. Let's stop a blink. A wee tot of brandy James?"

"Aye man, du'll never change. Good Health." James took a slug and handed it back. "I'm kind o guessing though du's up tae something Malcolm. I'm no sure we really need to be up here on da hill."

"See there behind us over the brim is the hill of Camb which runs up north a fair distance, and over there to the west is Muckle Swart Houll, stretching across to Whal Firth (or Whale Firth if you have an accent like me). It is rare bonny over there James. You would have walked between the hills here a few days back. Not very good sheep grazing though."

"Yes we did. Tanks to da aald pathway we got here. Dere's lots o birds and wildlife indeed. Da path was a bit rough and disappeared in places, but it was fine. I widna want tae try an fin my way through dere in da dark though. By the way, we call it knappan."

"What…the hills?"

"No, your accent…speaking all proper."

"Never heard that one before James. You and your Sheltie words…I think you just wind me up sometimes. Anyway… all of the Lumbister area is teaming with wildlife; more otters live here than humans. With the sheltered Firth on one side and the lochs up in the hills they thrive. Bonxies also thrive here at the expense of our lambs though. Bloody things them birds. I've been thinking James."

"Aha, I windered when da thinking bit wid arrive."

"Shush man and listen. I'll be away for three or four weeks, until Olivia and the bairns settle in Lerwick. It's a busy place getting to be is Lerwick and I am tempted to be looking around for some business ideas down there. So like I said, I will be away for a short while and need someone to look after things here. Not least the sheep and some feed to the horse and hens. Lambing season is nearly over but there are still quite a few to go yet up here in the hill and those damned bonxies will have them if left to their own. You can use the house until I return. I'll get in a load of food and there is enough eggs, hens and sheep to keep you both going for months."

"Weel, I don't ken whit to say. Du's obviously towt dis troo and I assume the weeminn will be having da sam conversation right noo. I am deeply grateful. It will gae wis some time tae plan wir next move, so it's an offer I can't refuse Malcolm. I'm pretty sure Babs will be delighted."

"The offer is very much for my own benefit, James and you just turned up at the right time. I have another little tempt though. You and I were good friends when we were boys; reared in different social backgrounds but blissfully unaware of any issues. Our parents are to be thanked for that. We could have been a different race or colour and wouldn't have noticed. We bonded and were mates from a young age. Then in our teens and beyond, that bond was tested as girls and ale got involved. We have tales that are better left untold… well I might stretch to telling our wives about the Communion Wine episode..!"

"Du worries me Malcolm. Du's going tae come oot wi something scary."

"No James, hopefully not. There is a little old house up Garth way. If I decide to sell Windhouse and the estate, which is more than likely, I might be persuaded to remove that property from the deeds."

"Mmmmm, I tink du needs tae feed me a bit mair information Malcolm. I can't see whit is in dat big square heed o yours."

"If you were minded to agree a deal, I think that house would make a fine place for you and Barbara to bring up your bairns."

"Weel noo dere's an offer. It wid indeed be a good start. I tink I ken the hoose…just north o Gutcher? I obviously need tae discuss wae Babs. However it soonds like we should jump at da chance. I don't ken hoo we might get started wi da rent though until I get up and going with Robbie Nisbet or possibly get wirsels some sheep or a boat to fish."

"Rent? I don't want rent, and once you get settled down to the cargo business your income will be fairly guaranteed… I think you should own it."

"You are going to sell me a house? Dat in feth! Dis is getting me flustered. Tanks but despite being awa for years I never learned hoo to sew up dese holes in my pockets. I dinna hae muckle spare cash tae brag aboot."

"Do not fret James. I'm not concerned. You will need every penny you have to see you through the first few months. Friends are worth more than money. We trust each other, so a deal can be struck that suits us both." Another swig from the hipflask put a glow on both their faces, "I think we should leave the bonxie hunt until later and get back to see what the ladies are saying."

As they jogged down the track James tentatively broached the scary room tale the girls had spoken about the day before.

"Och James, that's an old story me father used to tell just to scare the guests. He was a bit of a practical joker and mother used to say his pranks got a bit out of hand when he had too many drams in."

"Aye bit the bairns said dey geed into da room and it happened tae dem."

"Draughty old room that. The lamp must have blown out. The room was dark, the girls were scared. Nothing sinister James, just badly made windows and an easterly wind...."

The two friends walked on in silence but James was unconvinced. His thoughts however, were soon back to the house at Garth, or Gert as it was called locally.

That evening was predictibly going to be a bit of a celebration. Olivia prepared a mutton roast with all the trimmings, a feast that would provide James and Barbara with leftover meals for days. On retiring to the drawingroom the brandy decanter was refilled more than once while they yarned into the evening and daylight slowly disappeared. A few candles were lit and the atmosphere in the room was very peaceful. "Barbara told me about the beautiful poem you have given a tune James. Will you sing it to us?"

Supported by the copious amount of brandy James stood up, set his glass on the mantlepiece and cleared his throat. "Tanks to the genuine hospitality you have shown dese past few days and for presenting wis wae such a generous way forward, we hae a life changing plan. Hoo can I refuse. We hope we can repay your kindness wan day. Please forgive me if it comes out badly. I've never done this in front of an audience." James picked up Barbaras hand, looked into her eyes and sang *Grim Winter Was Howlin'*.

When he finished the room was quiet, Barbara sat with tears in her eyes. Olivia stood up and gave him a hug. "Thanks James, that was beautiful."

Malcolm refilled their glasess and sat down. "Right, enough of this lovie nonsense…lets lighten the conversation. I heard a grand story a few week ago, James. Your old pal Robbie and John Hendry…remember him?"

"Oh aye I do dat. He wis aye wan for his salty tales wis John Hendry."

"Well they were in the Bothy doon in the village here one night. The usual banter and bragging was going on amongst the punters. John Hendry, who had just arrived back from his deep sea voyages, was sitting beside Robbie.

> *"Du ever been across da Atlantic Robbie? Da seas are huge there Robbie…higher dan da mast dey are."*

"Aye, seen them John Henry. Big they are indeed."

"Du been in the Sooth Atlantic Ocean Robbie, roond Cape Horn? Du ever been dere Robbie? Ah min, biggest seas in da world. Twice the height o' da mast, gigantic dey are. Cape Horn is something else."

"Aye been there John Hendry man. Bit I'm tinkin' du's maybe no seen it all then. We were coming doon Bluemull Sound twa years back. Poor day it was…da seas were makin' big against da tide. In the valley o' the swell we were touching bottom, crushing crabs an limpets under da keel an on da tap o da waves whaar da white crests were being blown horizontally we were at such a height we could see da boats moored in Baltasound."

"I can hear him indeed Malcolm, and he would have finished off his reply with *"Laugh… I near bought me own beer"*. Aye haes da last word does Robbie. I don't tink he wid need to hae pitten his hand in his pocket again dat night."

Malcolm was up early next morning, harnessed the pony and trap and delivered a load of boxes and trunks to the pier. "The boat will be here in a couple of hours. We need to get ready and down there. Coats on everyone. Lets make tracks."

"I don't ken hoo du does it Malcolm…all dat drink last night. I could do wi a while in bed yet. My heed is splitting. I tink I've met my match wi yon French brandy. Could du see Robbie gets dis letter please? Tell him I'll meet up when he's on his next run up tae Yell. Dere will be a thousand questions an du'll manage tae fill him in on most o da details I'm sure."

"Yes that should be no bother. Just keep yourselves a low profile this next while and I'm sure it'll all settle down. Thanks again for looking after things.."

After a few hugs and cheerios the family strode down the road as the girls waved furiously back to James and Barbara standing in the doorway.

"Weel, Laird Malcolm Niven-Spence is one hell o a guy to have as a freend. Dat pack o cards are beginning tae look lik dey might be stacked in wir favour so far. Better get back in da hoose, Babs afore someen notices da door open. Whit a turn o events…"

Eighteen

Merran had gone to the cave the afternoon of their departure. As expected they were long gone but she brought home the flat stone that was the only evidence they had been there. *"Thanks mam. Love Mr&Mrs S. XX."*

"Well I suppose lass, du couldna lippen anything mair" said Jessie. No news is definitely good news at dis point. Da Laird is apparently still fuming, but I don't ken whit he can do if he wis tae catch up with dem. I am worried though what he might do tae de Merran. I guess he will be looking for da tree o you tagidder, probably heading sooth to Lerwick. I tink dat is whaar du has da advantage by bidin here wi me."

"Aye it's been fine here wae de Jessie. A bit cramped, but I'm no complaining. I tink it's time to speak wi Charles though. It will all have been a bit of a shock tae him and I tink he deserves wir version o tings. I certainly wild like tae hear his. I need tae move on in any case as da Laird will eventually catch up. Sam has predictibly been less dan supportive and I wouldna put it past him to do a bit o crawling if John Lawson offered him as much as a dram. We will be evicted fae Vigon noo for sure, including you Jessie. All I need is da claes on me back. I don't want tae take anything idder, and I tink we should mak a move wance it gets dark."

"I'm lived here aboots aa my life Merran and it'll be a wrench. But it certainly soonds like we need tae jump afore we are pushed. Du tinkin' to go back to Fetlar?"

"Weel It was a long while back I left da island and I still hae some relations dere Jessie. Dou would fit in weel. A new start. I'm dreamed o going back and I tink we might no hae mony options left."

"I'm an old burd noo Merran, and dis scares me a bit. But come on! Adventure was never far fae my sleepless nights. A bag o maet and a clean pair of knickers is all we need. Come on den. I'll support an help. Lets go."

"Oh Jessie du is a treasure and a true friend. Wha would believe yon waster I married is dy brother?"

"If I mind right, Merran dere was a young man in Fetlar afore Sam cerried de aff to Yell..."

"Whisht Jessie. Get dy knickers packed an we will be off in a blink."

In late May there is a lot of daylight hours in the far north, so it was late before the two women set off down the hillside. Taking an inland pathway to avoid Gloup they made their way towards Cullivoe, a route both of them had tramped many times over the years. They were tired by the time they came towards the village but could see a glow of light in the window of Greenbank.

"He's home Jessie."

Merran rapped on the door. It was not generally custom to knock so she lifted the latch and entered. The light was low. However, a figure was sitting in the only chair by the fire. "You there Charles?"

"Well if it isna da nearest thing I'm ever had to a midder in law. And Jessie! by god I'm honoured dis night.."

"Charles, can we come in? We need ti spik. I am no qualified tae apologise, however I hoop we can talk."

Charles lifted himself up and offered his chair and pulled another across the floor."Sit you both doon. Don't worry, I may no be sober but I'm no angry. I was angry for a time, den I ran oot o anger. I have been sad, den I ran oot o sad. I have been dortie. Do you ken what dortie is? Dortie is to sulk, be withdrawn and fold up into yourself. Well I don't tink I hae run oot o dat yet, but come sit doon. Tanks to aald Harry, though, I have turned a corner. Yes old Harry fae da shop sat down here dis morning and telt me a few tales. Tankfully he never tried to mak me laugh. He telled me I was a lucky buggar and a lot more besides. He's a wise old rogue is Harry. He has opened my eyes, something I should have been able to do on my own, but was too stupid. So Merran I think my dorty mood won't last much longer either. I do not hold any grudge wi Babs. She is a fine lass and I see noo da Laird was using me. He wis evicting families fae crofts and replacing them wi sheep. Much more profitible I can see, but at what cost tae all o wis? He needed a shepherd and I wis da gullible wan tae jump at da chance. Da Laird is creating division and if we let him continue dis wave o cruel evictions just to line his own pockets I will be as guilty. Yell will suffer. "

"My god Charles, what can I say?"

"I tink a drop o' nettle wine might be what you both need. My aald aunty Cissie aye dished out her nettle wine when she towtt anyeen needed an "*Ere o' Comfort.*" I feel drained by da past few days events and I'm managed to ease some of the pain dis evening, tanks to a few jars of Harrys ale, but I tink we need a drop of aunty Cissie's 'comfort'." He disappeared out the door with a slight stagger.

"Oh! My god Jessie. Whit did du tink o dat? Is he real? I hope he's no awa for a gun or something..."

They both jumped as Charles returned with a bottle and two glasses in hand.

"No fear ladies, I might look like a murderer, but even wae a drink in I widna hurt a hundiklok."

"Sorry Charles, I didna mean it. Dis is just so unexpected though. We towt we wad fin an angry person. I wouldna blame de, but dis has thrown me. I am so glad and I am so grateful. I ken it will hae been a huge shock an embarassment. Du is obviously a strong person... but whit next?"

"I'm no saying I am inclined to be civil towards James. I still hold some anger towards him. However I will no mak a scene. I wis being used by dat man up dere in da Haa and I hiv a letter ready tae tak ower wi my immediate resignation. Nae worries though as I hae only myself to keep and already hae my eyes on better tings dan sheep. Shetland has a lot to offer and I sense dere's big changes ahead."

They finished off several bottles of Cissie's potent wine and slept where they sat. Charles gave them a few old bannocks in the morning for their onward journey and left them to head south.

"Weel dat wis a night I'll never forget: I towt we would hae a three mile trudge fae Vigon last evening, hae a hells own row with Charles, dan sleep under da sheep dyke.... I tink he is made o' better stuff dan wae towt Merran. Dat aald widden chair wasna all dat comfy though mind, but da wine helped...ha ha!"

"He seems tae hae teen a' ting surprisingly well indeed Jessie. He was influenced by gifts and promises o better tings. A lesser mans brain wid still be under da spell o wir Laird. Being stood up has obviously shocked him, but no in a bad way. Wha wid have towt... I hoop it all works oot for him."

They walked on in the early morning and arrived a short while later in front of the Cullivoe shop. Merran opened the door with a TING.

"Ah! The Vigon ladies." Harry took Merran's elbow and escorted them through to the back. " I saw you come doon da track and guessed you might need a cup o tae. Must have been an early start comin doon fae Vigon dis caald morning?"

They didn't confess to where they had spent the night.

Harry was very supportive and understood their predicament. "You'll be needing somewye tae bide dis next while den ladies?"

"Aye. Please keep dis tae yoursel meantime Harry, but we are heading in da Gutcher direction, lookin to get across tae Fetlar…"

"Dere's a hoose I ken near Gutcher dat's been empty for a long while. It has a roof and windows and I tink some basic furniture wis left as weel. It might be worth bunking doon dere a while. I go past dat aald house every week delivering messages tae da neebourhood so could drop off some maet while du waits for tings tae settle doon. Lawson telt me da family are going tae be staying da summer near Edinburgh and will be leaving soon. I'll let de ken when he's awa and can sort oot a boat across tae Fetlar."

Nineteen

The first few weeks of Barbara and James's life in Windhouse was bliss: They remained indoors all day avoiding any passers-by and talked, shared each others trials and tribulations over the past ten years and fell in love all over again. As advised, they were careful to keep shutters closed at night and use the backdoor only. As far as everyone was aware the house was empty.

James went up the hill every evening to chase off bonxies and other predators and was delighted to spend time on his own just immersing himself in the peaceful and natural surroundings of the Niven-Spence estate. He arrived back one evening to find Barbara frantically pacing around the back yard. "James, thank goodnes. It's time we moved on. I'm really worried. An aald man stopped past this evening, knocking on da front door and asking for the Laird. I initially baed quiet indoors and ignored him. However he said he kent we were here and needed to talk, so I axed him to ging aroond da back and spoke wi him dere, keeping da door half closed atween us. He telt me he used to work for da Laird and had noticed da family wis awa, so was just checking up as he had seen lights on last evening. Windhouse, he said, is supposedly haunted and ower da years locals hae telt stories aboot mysterious lights movin aboot and idder strange tings happening in and aroond da house. He assured me it was nonsense and didna believe a word o it. Aabody liked to relate scary folk tales ower a winter fire and a jug of ale, so myth often became exaggerated and mixed into everyday life. He telt me dere was nothing for wis tae worry aboot, but he had been a peerie bit concerned when he saw the light in wan of da windows himsel. So he just needed to check it oot. *"for the Laird you understand"* he said a couple o times. He wished wis good fortune and withoot askin' my neem, he turned and walked back doon da way he came. I'm no sure why bit he wis very creepy James..."

"Well Babs, he does indeed sound a bit odd to say da least. I winder wha dat could be. Did he give a neem?"

"I tink maybe Dan or something like dat. I didna get him to say it again. He was awfull soft spoken and I already had to ax him a couple of times to repeat himsel."

"Well I suppose afore rumour spreads and we get more folk chapping at da door we probably should move indeed. Da lambing is all finished here anyway and Malcolm is due back in a few days. Da pony has enough water and da grass is plenty. Da hens can scratch aboot for twa days. I'll leave a note to say we have gone to check oot our new home at Gert. A quick tidy up da night, early bed and up first light o da morning."

James woke with Barbara sitting up in bed. It was still dark outside. The curtains were open and a full moon illuminated the room in black and white. Her eyes were wide open but she said nothing, just staring ahead. "Babs?... Babs, whit's wrong."

"Shhhh...", she whispered, "did you no hear it?"

"Hear whit?"

A floorboard creaked and sounded very near.

"That's it again..., dere's someen oot dere James."

James quietly lifted himself up on an elbow. "Just a creaky aald hoose" he whispered. "Da wind has shifted aroond tae da sooth. Da hoose will settle doon again afore morning.

"Why is du whispering den? Dere is something. Ging and look James, please, and tak dat staff wi de."

"All right Babs" James said not a little exasperated, and swung his legs over the bed. He placed his feet on the bare floorboards and gave a short intake of breath.

"Whit is it?"

"Bloody cold, that's whit it is."

James slowly tiptoed across the floor and gently turned the door knob. He pulled it quickly towards him and stood in the doorway looking out. Nothing. He peered into the darkness up and down the corridor and was about to turn back into the bedroom when he noticed a chink of light under a door, the door into the room the girls had been scared of. Quietly he crept towards it. The air felt as cold as the icy southern ocean and the hairs on the back of his neck were bristling. "Who's there?" he shouted. "Show yoursel, I hae a gun and will use it."

There was no answer. James put his hand to the door, turned the handle and sharply threw it open with a crash. The light went out.

Barbara screamed, "James, are you allright, James...?"

Standing in the doorway, walking stick waving above his head, he looked around the moonlit room which was enough to see there was nothing or no-one there, apart from a blanket in the corner. The window was swinging open.

James came back into the bedroom and Barbara clung tightly to him shivering as they stood in front of the bed. "I'm too fairt to lie doon. Someen or something wis in dat room. Whit dis du tink it wis? Will it come back?

"Weel it was no ghost, dat's for sure. Dey left a candle and a blanket ahint. Ghosts I'm sure don't need either. I tink whoever it wis got a bigger scare dan we did and will be miles away afore dey stop for a breath. Dey'll certainly no be back dis night, I'm sure o dat. I have locked da windows and doors forbye, so lets get some shut eye."

Daylight arrived two hours later, neither of them having slept another wink. They got dressed and pulled everything together including as much food as they could carry. A cup of warm tea later they set off along the well worn roadway north.

"I tink we should walk along da track Babs. We can no longer keep hiding. It is time Mr and Mrs Sinclair faced up to da world, so let today be the begining o wir new life."

"Windhouse wis a saviour James. Dy good friend Malcolm and Olivia were so hospitable. I look forward tae when we can meet up again and be able to repay dem in some way. It is indeed time for us to move on. We were way oot o wir depth there. I am no denying it was truly enjoyable while it lasted, a bit like I aye imagined a holiday would be like, except for lastnight. My God dat wis just gluffin. I'm still shaking. I couldna hae bidden dere anidder day. Aunt Jessie has a saying: *"Better a tin cup that's me ain than a silver cup that's borrowed"*. "So du's right, James my love, it's time tae face up tae wha we are, whatever the consequences. No more hiding. Today will be wir new beginning."

Olivia had given Barbara a large amount of clothes and shoes and together with food and other bags they struggled along the six mile track up to Garth. The weather was kind and they stopped frequently, so it was late afternoon when they passed the road to Gutcher and stopped. "Lets sit a minute Babs. Look doon dere lass. A bonny sight if ever I saw wan. Da loch o' Garth Malcolm called it. It gings wi da hoose so we will own dat as weel."

" Dis is just unbelievable James. I ken I said it afore, but still wonder if this is all a dream. I am fair puggled though wi all dis extra bags to carry. I must be getting aald."

"As we said Babs, today is da beginning. Everything afore was in preparation for whit comes next. Da hoose is joost a bit along here. Is du ready?"

"Ready James? I think I have been ready for ower ten years. Get yon bags on dy back. *"Glowerin i' the lum never filled the pot"*

"Well my bonnie lass, while du's quoting anidder o dy aald auntie Jessie's sayings I hae wan fae my aald grandad. I tink it suits dee grand."*Du disno bite sae sair as du girns".*

Barbara punched him in the arm looking up with a huge smile and strode on ahead.

Twenty

Smoke was rising from the chimney as they approached. "Dammit James, someen seems to be living here. Are we at the right hoose? Dis can't be Gert, Malcolm said da place wis empty."

The buildings of Garth were tucked down below the roadway so they could only see the back of the house with no doors or windows showing and no clues to who might be squatting inside.

"I'm sure dis is it. Lets go doon an see whit's goin on."

"All right James. Go you first. I'm tired, and I confess a peerie bit scared. I'll wait. Joost dinna tell me we hae tae walk much further."

James slowly crept around the gable end of the house, admiring the well built stonework, but also wondering what he might find around the front. There was suddenly a mighty crash and a woman jumped out through the doorway brandishing a stick, "Whit dis du want? No it can't be. It is… James!"

"Hells teeth woman! Jessie! Lay doon dat weapon wife. Du near killed me. Whit on Gods earth is du doing here?

"James, oh man, whit a relief. Where's Babs? Whaur is du been dis while? Whit's du doing here?"

"Wan question at a time Jessie. But first come roond here and see. Babs is waiting up at da gate."

"Merran, Merran, come oot. It's dem. Dey are here…"

The reunion was noisy, tears were mixed with laughter and hugs. James just stood back and watched as the three women cried together. They moved inside but there wasn't much daylight, the windows being draped in old hessian bags. The fire was soon glowing red and everyone settled down to have the much needed catchup.

"Lets start wi you mam and Jessie", Barbara said. "I'm been so worried aboot whit we left ahint, I wis selfish just up an leavin it all for you tae sort. It was all aboot me was it no?"

"My God lass no, I believe it's been a blessing. We hae so much tae tell. Right then. Lets start wi my escape fae da Haa."

"Mam… escape! Whit dis du mean?"

Both women rattled on into the evening with their tales since the day of the Contract Feast at Vigon, ending with their evening beside Charles Russland a few weeks ago.

"We have heard dat John Lawson an his wife Elizabeth hae geen sooth for da summer. Dere is still da on-going worry o da clearances, but many strong voices are coming forward in support o da crofters, an da community is getting tagidder, so I suspect da Laird might be in for a rough ride when he gets back."

"And fully deserved." They both concluded.

"So, Mr and Mrs Sinclair, your turn." Merran puffed up her old stained working dress and sat back in the chair. "I just can't wait any longer to fin oot whit you have been up to. No sleeping very rough by the looks of you both."

They took turns in relating their story, bit by bit, from when James set foot back in Yell, to Barbara fleeing to the cave, the marriage, their trek over the hills and their most unexpected long stay at Windhouse, then finally up to Garth. They stopped briefly at one point to boil up tea and eat some of the food they had packed. Lighting a few candles and throwing more peats on the open fire the story telling carried on.

"Windhouse is a funny place Babs. Whit did du tink? Jessie asked.

"Weel it was really fine for maist o da time", Barbara told them. "we couldna hae been better looked efter.

"However Da bairns, Charlotte and Vaila, were very unsettled aroond bed time an I felt a bit concerned for dem. Dere was wan room dey were scared o."

"Go on den", James said. "Might as well tell dem aboot da streen."

"Well it kind o started wi an aald man stopping past…"

Barbara finished the story and the four of them sat in silence.

"Da aald man du speaks aboot, Babs, whit did he look like?" asked Jessie quietly.

"Weel, he wis kindo short, wearin an aald flat cap and no had a shave for days. His teeth, though I couldna stop looking at his teeth. Only two, tobacco stained pegs, in the bottom o his mouth. He kind o whistled when he spoke."

Jessie tensed up "Is du sure Babs…aboot his teeth?"

"Of coorse, Jessie. Whit's wrong?"

"Wis he called Daniel?"

"Something like dat I tink…dis du ken him?"

"I tink I might Babs. Daniel or Dan, used to be great entertainment at da bothy in da village. He had a story for every occasion. He often sat on da highest chair an after a few rums wid sing a ballad or two. Any newcomer wid get da tale o his teeth, or redder his lack o teeth and hoo he lost dem off Greenland when harpooning a shark." *"Put up wan hell of a fight, left me wi only four teeth in me heed, da damned fish. Biggest trouble is da two on the top are at da back, and da two on the boddam are in da front. I can no longer eat a lump o beef. 'have to get da wife to chow it first den give it back! Ha ha..."*

"Soonds a right character. Probably wis him indeed," said Barbara.

"I'm no sure whit tae say. I don't want tae gluff de any more. Dere will be an explanation. Hooever, Daniel died five years ago. He fell aff a scaffold while fixing da roof at Windhouse. So it couldna been him could it...?"

They all sat in silence a long while, conversation dried up. They were all exhausted and Merran threw some blankets around as everyone huddled up in chairs and slept... the peat fire embers disappeared and the candles burned out.

The morning sun was beaming into the cottage when James pulled down the ragged cloth from the windows. "Let there be light!" he said as he bundled up the old blackout hessian and threw it into the fireplace. He donned his boots, laced them up and kissed Barbara on the top of her head before disappearing out the door.

"I sense we hae wan very happy James dis morning." beamed Barbara.

"Well my dears" Merran said, "I tink wan more day here and da two o us aald burds should be able to get a boat ower to Fetlar. I'm teld da old family croft hoose might need some wark, but cherish the challenge."

"Indeed Merran. Dere's nothing left for me noo in Yell. So I'm happy tae mak a new beginning, like dese bairns are doin' here. I hoop the house in Fetlar is a big een though. By the twinkle in dy eye I tink we might hae a visitor or two!"

"Da poor Fetlar folk don't ken what's aboot tae hit dem," chuckled Barbara, still wrapped up in her blanket.

"Ah Babs, whit a sequence o events. James will be aff wi Robbie delivering cargoes aroond da isles, and du haes Gert here to mak into dy home. My god, I'm so happy for de. Da story tellers will thrive on dis fireside yarn for years." Merran turned and looked at her daughter. "Du's lookin a preerie bit badly da day though lass. It's been tough. A long struggle. Is du all right? Du surely can't be....?"

"Oh mam, I was never able tae hide onyting fae de. I'm been a bit poorly for twa days noo. I tink I might be gan tae hae a bairn…"

"Fegs lass. A bit soon tae be sure of dat I would tink." Jessie piped up as she scraped out ashes from the hearth.

With her back turned she didn't see mother and daughter exchange a smile.

*********** THE END ***************

Dictionary.

a braw few: a large number.

abeun;   above.

ahint;   behind.

athoot;   without.

ax: ask.

badly: ill.

bairn;   child.

banns;   proclimation to announce a marriage in the church.

beating flux;   beat your arms around your body to warm up.

blyde;   happy or fond.

bolster: long/double pillow.

Bosie;   hug.

braaly: very.

breex;   trousers.

bursten: a meal made from corn.

claes;   clothes.

da;   the.

dat in feth;   good grief!

dee;	you.
dem;	them.
dey;	they.
dort(y);	sulk(y).
dou'll;	you will.
dreech;	damp/drizzlie weather.
drookled;	soaking wet
dungarees;	jeans/trousers.
dy;	your.
dysel;	yourself.
ebb;	exposed area of beach when the tide is out.
ee noo;	at the moment.
errand;	message/small task.
ething;	something.
faeder;	father.
faering:	gift.
fantin;	hungry.
fegs;	expression of surprise.
flix;	fright.

foy;	social gathering.
gansey;	jumper.
Ging(s);	go(es).
gluff / gluffin:	fright / scaring.
gone by his mind;	irrationally very angry.
goonie;	nightgown.
guk;	stupid fellow.
hundiklok;	winged beetle.
idders;	others.
joost;	just.
kirn:	small barrel.
kraeg;	cliff.
lippened;	expected.
lookin' badly;	looking unwell.
lug;	ear.
maet;	food.
mair;	more.
makin';	making.
mam;	mother/mum.

mirknen;	darkening / evening twilight.
muckle boady:	large quantity.
muckle hurd:	big boulder/stone.
neep;	turnip.
onkerry;	carry on.
onywye:	anywhere.
oxter;	armpit.
Pawns:	guarantee of intenmtion deposit.
peerie (peedie):	small.
pheesic;	medicine.
poorly;	unwell.
poots(ie):	sulk.
Precentor:	Church official.
press;	cupboard.
scarf/scarfie	cormorant.
scurtful:	armful.
selkie man:	a seal, when removing his seal skin turnes into a man.
simmit;	vest.
sixareen:	traditional Shetland boat with six oars.

smooriken;	kiss.
snifter;	dram/drink.
somewey;	somewhere.
speil;	verbal delivery.
start;	short time.
staff;	walking stick.
streen (da);	lastnight/yesterday.
taak;	take.
tae;	tea.
tang;	seaweed.
tink;	think.
t'ither;	the other.
tize;	persuade.
towt;	thaught.
Trow;	troll/fairy/elf.
trow;	through.
wae;	with.
wis;	us.

witter (gone in a); become complicated/stuck.

ACKNOWLEDGEMENTS

A huge thanks to everyone who helped get this book to print:

My loving wife Elsie for supporting and keeping me motivated.

To sister Linsey Nisbet for her expert proof reading and providing the Shetland dialect input.

Brother in law Andrew Nisbet and Robert Henderson for relating the story, identifying the cave and for keeping me right with local geography.

Wilma Henderson, and Colin Dickie for supplying invaluable historical information and factual correctness.

Everyone else for the help and encouragement when I was needing a boost.

Mike Cooper (Molly Mack) for the artwork, the words, and for being there.

I couldn't have done it without you.

Printed in Great Britain
by Amazon